DEDICATION

TO ALL THOSE WHO NEVER GIVE UP

ACKNOWLEDGMENTS

I love the use of quotes when appropriate. The series THE DEFIANT will be about those souls who refuse to give in and are those who struggle. So that being said, this quote from President Theodore Roosevelt seems fitting and will set a tone for the book you're about to read. – John W. Vance

"It is not the critic who counts; not the man who points out how the strong man stumbles, or where the doer of deeds could have done them better. The credit belongs to the man who is actually in the arena, whose face is marred by dust and sweat and blood; who strives valiantly; who errs, who comes short again and again, because there is no effort without error and shortcoming; but who does actually strive to do the deeds; who knows great enthusiasms, the great devotions; who spends himself in a worthy cause; who at the best knows in the end the triumph of high achievement, and who at the worst, if he fails, at least fails while daring greatly, so that his place shall never be with those cold and timid souls who neither know victory nor defeat."

PROLOGUE

The smell of fresh tilled earth was one of Abigail's favorite smells. The richness of the soil in her garden had produced one good crop after another and had been the lifeblood for her family. Taking pride in a hard day's work, she finally noticed her daughter, Alexis, wasn't outside anymore. Needing a break and curious as to where her thirteen-year-old had gone to, she set the hoe down and walked towards the small ranch house she and Alexis called home.

On her way inside she grabbed a pail and filled it from the well. Each time she pumped the handle a steady stream of cool, clean water flowed. Unable to resist, she grabbed the ladle that hung from the pump and scooped herself some water.

The spring sun was descending behind the horizon, and soon she'd need to be preparing dinner for her and Alexis. Tired and still curious as to Alexis' whereabouts, she went inside.

For the two of them the house was a bit large, but it was theirs and she felt fortunate to have a safe place, especially one with land. On her way to the kitchen she passed the den and stopped. The light streamed in through a large window and was hitting the leather desk chair just right. Her mind raced back to a happier time when the chair held the man she loved. In her mind's eye she could see Samuel sitting and working on a piece of legislation or drafting a speech. She didn't miss the days of being a politician's wife, especially the wife of a president, but she'd gladly give anything to relive the worst of those days just to be in his arms again.

The weight of the full pail began to pull on her arm, so she headed into the kitchen. A large ceramic bowl sat on top of the brown granite counter next to the large basin sink. She filled the bowl with the cool water; with a washcloth she cleaned the day's work from her hands and arms. The availability of instant hot water was a luxury she missed from the days she spent in Austin with Samuel. As she began to wipe the grime from her face, a loud crash stopped her.

"Alexis, is everything all right?" she called out.

No reply.

The scampering of feet now echoed down the hall from her bedroom.

Concerned that something might be wrong, she reached into a drawer and pulled out a small revolver. Firmly gripping the pistol, she made her way down the long hallway towards the closed door of her bedroom.

A shadow raced back and forth underneath the door.

"Alexis, is everything all right?" she again called out.

Still no reply.

At the door she paused and took hold of the rubbed bronze handle and turned. The handle clicked and opened.

More scampering came from the room.

Abigail's heart was pounding. She hadn't encountered trouble on her property in years, and even though where they lived was relatively safe, they lived on the outskirts of the city. Too far for help to come if she called, hers was a life of self-reliance, and this was a moment she wanted nothing more than a small army of people to be available.

Abigail flung the door open.

Alexis was in front of the opened closet, hastily putting papers and small keepsakes back in a large box.

"Alexis, what are you doing?"

The weight of guilt overcame her. With her shoulders slumped forward and head bowed, she only said, "I'm sorry."

"What are you doing in here?" Abigail asked, stepping into the room. Not wanting Alexis to see the revolver, she quickly stuffed it in her back pocket.

"I wanted to—"

"You made a mess," Abigail snapped as she went to her knees and began to examine the objects on the floor.

"I'm sorry."

"You should be. If you want to see something, ask me."

Alexis didn't move. Her thick brown hair concealed her face and the embarrassment of being caught going through her mother's belongings.

Abigail's irritation quickly dissipated. She reached out and lifted Alexis' face.

Tears slowly streamed down Alexis' cheeks with a few clinging to her chin.

"Oh, honey, you don't need to cry," Abigail said.

3

"I just need to know," Alexis whimpered.

Abigail looked into the deep blue eyes of her daughter. Alexis was a beauty, tall, slender, with an angelic face. Her large blue eyes twinkled when she was happy, but when she was overcome with sorrow, like now, they showed it. Abigail always knew how Alexis was feeling because her eyes were truly windows into her soul.

Abigail brushed Alexis' hair behind her ears and pulled her close for an embrace, but she stopped her just short and asked, "Mom, who's my real father?"

"What?"

"Who's my real father?"

"Your dad is your father. Why would you ask such a question?"

"Cousin Timmy told me that. He said Daddy wasn't my real dad. He said that my real dad died in the revolution."

Abigail recoiled from the question.

Seeing her response, Alexis pressed further. "Is it true?"

It was true, and Abigail knew the day would come when the truth would have to be revealed. She just wanted to coordinate the timing, but life had a way of showing that control was a myth. Abigail wanted to lie, but maybe this was the time. Alexis was thirteen, and in this world she was more mature and capable than when she was her age.

Alexis took her hand and asked sweetly, "Mom, please understand I'll always look at Daddy as my dad, but ever since Timmy mentioned it, I haven't been able to stop thinking about it. I need to know."

Shaking her head in frustration at the situation she was in, Abigail said, "When I see Cousin Timmy, I'll give him a piece of my mind."

"Is it true?"

"It is true. I'm sorry I didn't tell you before, but it's very complicated," Abigail answered, resting her back against the large wooden footboard of the bed.

"Who was my father?"

"The answer is easy, I can just give you a name, but you deserve more than that. You deserve to know the entire truth."

Alexis turned her body and faced her mother. Her eyes were wide with anticipation of the great reveal.

Abigail exhaled deeply. Her mind raced with just where to start the story of who her father was and how it came to be that Samuel Becker took over and, more importantly, why it was kept secret.

"In order to give everything context, I need to start with your granddad."

"Granddad? What does he have to do with this?" she asked, curious and confused.

"He has a lot to do with it. It was because of him that your father and I met. I was sixteen when I met your biological father."

Alexis touched Abigail's hand and caressed it. "What was his name?"

Abigail rested her entire weight against the footboard and gave in to her memories. A slight grin graced her face as she thought back to the day she met him.

"Mom, what was his name?"

"Luke, his name was Luke Summers."

"Luke Summers, hmm, I like it."

"He was so handsome and charming," Abigail said softly.

"Do you have a picture?" Alexis asked.

Abigail stood up and walked into the closet, stepping over the spilled contents of the box. She rummaged and came out with a small cedar box.

Alexis could barely contain herself.

Abigail sat back down and cradled the box. She looked at her sweet daughter and said, "You look just like him. There's not a day that goes by that I don't think about him. I used to joke that you were his twin. Your dark hair, fine features and those eyes, those are his eyes."

"Do you still love him?" Alexis asked.

"I never stopped loving him. He was taken from me, from us far too soon," Abigail answered as she nervously tapped the top of the box with her thumbs.

"Can I see him?"

The cedar box opened with a creak. Abigail fished through the contents and took out an old smart phone. She pressed the power button, but it didn't turn on. "It's dead; I need to charge it."

Alexis looked at the device and chuckled.

"These things used to be our lifeblood before the lights went out," Abigail said, holding the phone. She stood and left the room. A moment later she returned and sat back down.

"No other photos?"

"No one really developed their pictures back then. We

never thought we'd need real photographs. So many people thought the world wouldn't change, but it did. You know the history, but you don't really know our family history and how we came to be in Oklahoma. Now that the cat is out of the bag, you need to know all of it, the good and the bad."

Alexis scooted closer with the anticipation of hearing it all.

"It all began when I was sixteen, and if it hadn't been for your granddad, you and I wouldn't be here. You see, your granddad did whatever it took to keep me safe, and when you were born, he ensured you'd be raised in safety," Abigail said, then stopped. It had been years since she had thought about those days.

"Mom, you okay?"

"Yeah, I'm fine. I just haven't thought about it in such detail. I mean, I think about those days and they've made me the person I am today, but to recount it brings back a lot of emotion."

"You don't have to."

"No, I do. You found out about your biological father in the wrong way. You're a young woman now and you deserve to know the truth."

Alexis gripped Abigail's hand tightly.

"Like I said, you need to know all of it to understand why we did what we did," Abigail said as she took her other hand and caressed Alexis' face.

The years had been fair to Abigail. She didn't have too many wrinkles for a woman in her late thirties, but the gray hairs weren't as kind. She liked to refer to them as silver versus gray and they streaked her straight black hair.

Alexis had asked many times where she had gotten her blue eyes, as Abigail and Samuel had dark brown. Before, Abigail just told her eye color skipped generations and that her great grandfather had light eyes. This of course was a lie, but a useful one until now.

Alexis sat eagerly waiting for the story of her life to begin, the grip on her mother's hand steady in its firmness.

"I know you've heard me say it before, but our lives are touched by many people. All along the way, we've had the pleasure of meeting some great people and unfortunate occasions we encountered some unsavory ones. But without a doubt, if you were to follow a path back in time to how this all came to be, you'd end up with your granddad, my daddy. Unfortunately, you never got to meet him, but he was a strong and determined man. Mom used to joke and say he was a prophet. He knew that one day we'd have a day of reckoning, and it came; he just knew that one day our world would end and many people wouldn't know how to handle the fall. Granddad was prepared, though, and he did some unorthodox things. Some might consider his actions harsh, but he did so to keep me and your grandmother alive. We owe our lives to him." Abigail paused, took a deep breath and continued. "The beginning of the world you know started with an end to the last one. Let me take you back to the day the lights went out."

CHAPTER ONE

"To be prepared is half the victory." – Miguel de Cervantes

Carlsbad, CA, United States
Present Day

Sweat streamed down Nicholas McNeil's chiseled face as a broad smile grew. Standing like a statue atop the mountain, he overlooked his community and the ocean beyond in the far distance. His morning trail runs gave him a boost and started his days off strong.

The strong aroma of sage and dirt hit his nostrils. He breathed in deeply through his nose, taking it all in. The richness of his surroundings helped alleviate the stresses that riddled his life beyond what just a run would.

The mountaintop was the halfway point for his runs and was the highlight of each run. The vistas were magnificent, but more importantly, it gave him a perspective of his world.

A successful entrepreneur and wealth manager, Nicholas strived to never forget where he came from. His humble beginnings and lack of a formal education would have spelt doom for many, but Nicholas never allowed conventional constructs or negative thoughts to stop him from achieving what he wanted.

His arms bore the scars of his first adventure as a man, the Marines. Upon his completion of high school, he followed in his older brother's footsteps and joined the service. While his brother had been an Army Ranger, he joined the Marines, a sign that he had some independence. Some would have considered going into battle something to dread, but he was excited when his unit was deployed to Saudi Arabia to defend it from Iraq. For him what followed was months of boredom, but when the ground combat began he only saw two days before being wounded by mortar fire outside of Kuwait International Airport. His wounds were significant enough that eleven months later he was medically discharged. He missed the Marines, but Nicholas was never one to focus on the negative and besides he still carried pieces of shrapnel in him. He considered them a reminder and a strange memento from a different life. Twenty years had gone between the day he exited the hospital with his entire life stuffed into a sea bag and now, a father of a teenager and employer of fifteen people.

He pulled the sweat-stained ball cap off and wiped his forehead. The cool morning air felt good against his warm wet skin. Losing track of time, he unzipped his jacket pocket and pulled out his mobile phone. After pressing the home button, he expected to see the screen illuminate, but it remained dark.

"Hmm, I swore I charged it," he said out loud as he pressed the on/off button at the top of the phone.

The phone remained dark.

He looked up towards where the sun might be in the

east, but the thick clouds produced from the marine layer hid it.

He turned to head back home when a loud crash echoed through the mountains and valleys. The sound of crunching metal came from the main road that fed into his neighborhood.

"Ouch, not a good way to start the morning," he said to himself as he began his descent.

The trailhead was conveniently located a hundred feet from the intersection where the gates to his community were. Not thinking too much of the cars sitting at the light, he reached out and hit the crosswalk button.

His thoughts gravitated back to the tasks before him later that day. First was a conference call with a client back east, and second was a meeting with a representative from Goldman Sachs. If he could score their business, he'd add a large amount of assets to his already large portfolio of managed funds. He ran through that meeting from the first handshake until the eventual agreement that his firm was perfect. Nicholas liked to visualize all of his meetings this way; he thought it prepared him and aligned his subconscious mind to what he wanted to happen.

The car door of an SUV at the stoplight opened and a woman stepped out, cursing.

This caught his attention and pulled him from his thoughts. He thought it peculiar she was standing outside of her car.

Then a man got out of the car next to hers. He was holding his mobile phone high in the air and then shook it.

A deep vertical line formed when Nicholas pressed his

brows together. He watched these people, unsure of why they were outside their cars. A question hit him: what were the odds that both their cars weren't working.

He looked at the crosswalk sign and saw it was dark. He pressed the button repeatedly and nothing happened. His curiosity took over as he stepped out onto the road and looked in either direction. What he saw confused him. What was usually a busy dual-lane road was at a standstill. Cars riddled the lanes in both directions, all frozen in place, some with their hoods up.

An unsettled feeling came over him. Something was wrong. He didn't know what it was, but what he was seeing was something he'd never seen before.

Over the past year and a half Nicholas had been insuring his family's ultimate survival by gathering resources like extra water and long-term food supplies. All his life he had prepared financially, but the last few years he'd seen enough warning signs in the economy and geopolitically to know that the status quo would not remain like it was. This paranoia met with what he was witnessing and created a panic in him.

He sprinted across the street and towards the pedestrian gate of his community, Rancho Del Sur, a collection of over two hundred Tuscan- and Mediterranean-style homes. He unlocked the gate and swung it wide open. As he ran past the gatehouse, he overheard the guard reassure a neighbor about the power outage.

"Sir, as soon as our phones are back up, I'll call triple A."

Nicholas' heart was pounding furiously in his chest as

he put one foot in front of the other, inching closer to his house. The realization that something horrible and universal had occurred was reinforced as he saw more neighbors outside their homes than he had ever seen. Many were walking around, mobile phones in their hands and the hoods of their cars up.

"Nic, do you know what's wrong?" an elderly woman hollered at him as he ran past.

He stopped in front of her. "I don't know. I've been gone, out for a run, but it looks like many people's cars aren't working," he said.

"My phones don't work either and the electricity is off. Phil, the young attorney who lives next to me, can't get his car started; he says it must be some terrorist attack or something."

"He may be right. Now if you'll excuse me, I need to go home, check on my family," Nicholas said and continued his run back.

He made the front door but couldn't get the key to line up with the lock, as his hands were shaking. Taking a moment, he took a couple deep breaths and said, "Relax." He inserted the key and unlocked the door.

Inside he encountered the same silence he had left an hour ago.

Up the stairs he went.

In the master bedroom his wife, Becky, lay sleeping. "Becky, get up, come on, time to get up."

Becky, his wife of eighteen years, mumbled, "Huh?"

"Get up. Something's happened; I need you to wake up," he ordered, a slight panic in his voice. He bolted down the hall towards his daughter, Abigail's room.

Sleep had been something Becky hadn't been able to have for years; in fact, she couldn't remember the last time she had a good night's sleep. Since before giving birth to Abigail over sixteen years ago, sleep had left her life, and she swore it was never coming back. At first she blamed Abigail, but now there was no one to blame but herself. Most evenings were spent lying in bed streaming television shows on her iPad until the early morning hours.

Nicholas had told her it was stimulus that kept her from the much-needed sleep, but she argued with him.

She didn't disagree, but she'd never admit it. Their relationship had gotten to a sad point that she didn't want him to be right about many things.

"Abby, get up!" Nicholas shouted down the hallway of their two-story Tuscan-style home.

Abigail didn't move.

"Abby, get up. Something is wrong!" Nicholas barked as he knocked on her locked door. "And no more locking the door."

"Okay, okay, I'm getting up!" Abigail hollered.

Nicholas marched back towards his room and found Becky slowly moving around.

"Something bad has happened. We need to get ready to leave," Nicholas said his voice an octave higher than normal.

"Whoa, easy, you're way too intense for so early," Becky commented.

"This isn't a joke, and trust me, something bad has happened."

"Is the power out?" Becky grunted as she tapped repeatedly on the light switch in the bathroom.

Nicholas walked in behind her and said, "That's one part of it, but cars aren't working, my phone is dead. Um, wait a minute," he said and quickly left the room. "It's the same."

"Same what?" Becky asked, her attention mainly on her reflection in the mirror.

"My phone is dead, yours is too, and so is your iPad."

"Maybe we didn't charge them."

"You're not listening to me. No one's car is working. This is some sort of attack against us."

"Honey, I told you, buy whatever survival stuff you want. You don't have to justify it with me," Becky said, splashing cool water on her face. Her comment referenced her disregard and sometimes contempt for Nicholas' recent purchases of food, water and equipment primarily used by preppers and survivalists. She didn't want anything to do with it, as she thought it silly and especially hated it when he would openly discuss his new views and hobbies with old friends. Often he would see her rolling her eyes and chiming in on the mocking and making fun of him with their skeptical friends. Her ambivalence had reached a critical point for Nicholas so that he stopped discussing things with her and just did whatever he wanted. This disappointed him, as he thought it would be fun if they could do it together, but he realized that after eighteen years of marriage, sometimes you didn't grow together on all things.

Nicholas shook his head and barked, "Becky, when

you're done, meet me downstairs."

San Diego, CA

"Sophie! Get up; wake up. We're late!" Bryn Salinger yelled as she scrambled around her bedroom getting dressed.

Sophie cringed each time her sister yelled. Unable to move due to a pounding headache, she put a pillow over her head. Their last night together had been spent in typical fashion, drinking till the bars closed in Pacific Beach.

Bryn, half dressed, stormed into the living room of her tiny apartment to discover Sophie still lying on the couch with the pillow covering her face. She walked over, snatched the pillow and tossed it across the room. "Get up; we're late. The clock isn't working, and by the looks of it outside, it's well past eight. Now get up!"

"Argh, my head hurts." Sophie sighed.

Bryn hurried back into the bedroom. "Where's my phone? Have you seen it?"

Sophie sat up and rubbed her eyes, looked and saw her own phone and said, "Found mine." She pressed the home button, but nothing happened. She then hit the power button, but still the phone was dark. Unable to get it to work, she tossed it back on the table and fell back onto the sofa.

Bryn rushed back out of the bedroom and into the kitchen. "Where's my phone?"

"Bryn, don't sweat it. I'll take a later flight. There has

to be more than one flight to San Francisco."

"I have other stuff to do today than be your chauffeur!" Bryn shot back.

"Go, I'll take a cab," Sophie answered as she fell onto her side into the thick cushions of the couch. "Hey, did I get that guy's number last night?"

"Come on. Get up. I thought you said—"

"Bryn, chill out. I'll take a cab and get a later flight, just leave me some cash."

"Here it is!" Bryn exclaimed when she found her phone buried in her purse. She saw the screen was dark and tried to turn it on, but the phone remained dark. "Damn, it's dead." She hooked it up to the charger and walked into the bathroom. When she hit the light switch, the light stayed dark. "Oh, come on!"

"Bryn, please stop yelling about everything. My head is pounding."

"What is going on? There must be a power outage," Bryn said, then began to walk around the apartment, hitting every light switch only to find that the power was out. She walked to her phone, unplugged it and said, "I'll be right back. I'm going to run to the car and charge this."

Opening the door brought in the late morning light and illuminated the reality that something else had happened. From the second-floor balcony she had a bird's-eye view of the apartment complex parking lot, and there she saw the beginnings of what would become a very long day. Across the expansive lot was car after car with its hood up; people were milling around everywhere. Some were talking; others were under the hoods of the cars, fruitlessly attempting to get the cars operational. She hadn't seen so many of her fellow neighbors collectively gathered much less all talking among themselves, ever.

Her neighbor, a young woman named Crystal, pushed by her, holding her mobile phone up and cursing, "What the fuck!"

Bryn leered at her as she rudely didn't even take notice that she had brushed by her. Under her breath, she said, "I hate you."

"Oh, come on!" Crystal barked. She stopped looking at her phone and began to walk back to her front door when she took notice of Bryn and asked, "Is your phone working?"

"No."

"What's going on here? This is such bullshit!" Crystal growled. She was a tall, lean and attractive girl who Bryn remembered was her age, twenty-eight. She always kept her hair long, a platinum blonde. It hung down to the middle of her back and was rarely ever pulled back.

Bryn swore she was either a stripper or escort based upon the way she dressed. She either wore yoga pants or was dressed up like she was clubbing it; either way, Bryn never saw her wear the boring and conservative attire she had to endure as a human resources assistant. However, the main reason she thought she did what she did was because of the endless parade of older men, some in their fifties, heading to her apartment. But then again, what did she know. Maybe she was just looking for a sugar daddy. Bryn found herself judging her but soon would back off when she realized she hadn't lived a life without sin and sometimes people did whatever they felt they had to, but then again, she just couldn't imagine stripping or selling her body.

"Hello?" Crystal said loudly.

"No, I don't know what's going on," Bryn finally answered her; she wasn't paying much attention to Crystal, as she was more focused on trying to figure out what strange thing had occurred.

Bryn turned and went back inside her darkened apartment. She tossed open the shades, allowing the morning sun to chase away the darkness.

"Really?" Sophie screamed as she turned away from the light.

"Get up, something's happened, get up!" Bryn exclaimed as she hurried into her bedroom to grab some shoes.

Sophie sat up and looked out the large front window and squinted, "Oh, come on, just let me sleep. This isn't a big deal. I'll take a cab."

Bryn came back into the room and said, "I don't think that's going to happen."

"Why are you being such a bitch this morning?"

"I'm not; I'm being a big sister. Now get up. We need to find out if our car is working," Bryn said as she snatched the car keys from a small bowl on the nightstand next to the front door and went back outside.

Sophie looked at her and said, "You go do that." She fell back onto the couch and covered her face with the blanket.

Sycamore Grove, the apartment complex Bryn called home, consisted of twelve two-story tan stucco-sided buildings spread across three and a half acres. Each building housed twenty apartments, with each side having ten, five up and five down. The buildings formed a U-shape; a large swimming pool and community center were positioned in the middle. Concrete sidewalks connected all the buildings and their amenities. Surrounding all the buildings were small patches of grass, flowering plants, trees and shrubs.

For San Diego standards, the complex was older, having been built in the 1990s, and the rents were modest, which fit into Bryn's tight budget. She came from a well-to-do family but refused to take any money from her mother, as their relationship had become estranged since she left home at eighteen. For Bryn's mother, the only thing she could do was give money, but what Bryn had always wanted was her time, which for her was too much to give. Bryn prided herself on being able to survive without her mother's money, and even though she dreamt of living larger, she'd gladly wait till *she* could make it happen.

Bryn made her way down to the parking lot that fronted her building with her keys in hand. She pressed the fob to unlock her bright green Kia Soul, but the lights didn't flash like they normally did. That was her first clue that something was wrong and she had succumbed to the same fate as others had. She flipped the key out and inserted it into the door and manually unlocked the car. The second sign her car had become a victim was the dome light didn't turn on. She climbed in, put the key in, and just before she turned it, she paused to say a little prayer,

"Please turn on, please." She turned the key, but nothing happened, not even a click. The car was dead. She tried again and again, foolishly hoping that with a random attempt the engine would roar to life, but it didn't. Frustrated and now getting scared, she rested her head back, closed her eyes and began to think about what could cause something like this. She physically jumped when a tap on the window startled her; she looked and couldn't make out who it was. She opened the door and got out, now irritated by whoever startled her. When she saw it was Matt Bessner, the thirty-something-year-old single geek who lived downstairs, she barked, "You scared the shit out of me!"

"I'm sorry; I saw you and thought—"

She slammed the car door and began to walk back to her apartment, ignoring him.

Matt was thirty-three, but by the way he dressed, Bryn joked that he looked like he was thirteen. When not wearing his blue Best Buy polo, he could be seen sporting a variety of comic book character or *Star Wars* T-shirts.

Bryn found him annoying; he was constantly trying to start up a conversation with her. She couldn't escape him; whether she clearly looked busy or was in a hurry, he felt compelled to talk to her. She wanted to forgive him, as she knew he wasn't a bad person, but she just couldn't help but find his joyful persona a bit irritating. Some days she'd feel sorry for him, as she would see him walk to his car tugging awkwardly at one of his T-shirts in an attempt to hide his chubby belly. Behind his black glasses, unshaven stubble and coffee-stained teeth, she thought that if someone were to give him guidance, he just might clean up nicely.

When he wasn't working, Matt could be found in one of three places, at home playing video games, at the movie theater, or at the local Bennigan's with his friends. It wasn't that Matt lacked the ability or talent to work beyond his customer service representative position at Best Buy, he didn't care. His main interests in life were games, science fiction and comic books. His job afforded him a place to keep up with the latest gadgets, and he loved the job, without a doubt.

Seeing she was upset, he again apologized, "I'm sorry, really."

"Leave me alone, Matt."

"Don't be mad at me, I really didn't mean to scare you," he begged now as he followed her.

"Matt, please leave me the fuck alone. Unless you know what's happened, I don't have time," she barked, holding her hand up as she strode away, not looking at him.

He stopped and loudly said, "I know what happened."

This comment caused her to stop in her tracks; she turned and asked, "Really?"

"Um, sure. I mean, I don't know for sure, but I have a really good guess," he now said sheepishly.

"Go ahead."

"It's an EMP."

"A what?"

"Electromagnetic pulse, it knocks out everything electronic. You see…" he said as he slowly walked towards her. His head was swimming with the details of all the shows, movies and video games that utilized such weapons.

THE DEFIANT: GRID DOWN

"This isn't one of your science fiction, comic book things, is it?"

"No, no, not at all, ahh, this has all the characteristics of an EMP for sure."

"How do you know?"

He knew his answer might elicit scorn, but he said it anyway, "I've seen movies and such, and—"

Bryn cut him off. "This isn't one of your science-fiction movies."

"EMPs are real. In fact, they're more science fact than fiction, but my understanding is," he said then paused.

"What?"

"An EMP doesn't typically knock everything out. I mean, it's not typically universal. Small devices not close to the blast radius would still work, like our phones, but they don't, unless we were right below the blast."

"Blast?"

"Yeah, blast. I mean, this couldn't have been a CME; that wouldn't have taken out the phones, only an EMP would do that," he said. His speech increased in tempo as he rattled off detail after detail about EMPs and their capabilities.

Bryn watched him as he divulged everything he knew about an EMP and what it could do. He cited different movies, commenting on how some were accurate in their depiction of EMPs and criticized others. He referenced video games she had never seen, played, much less ever heard of to bolster his knowledge of EMPs. Everything he was saying went right over her head, but if anyone would know what could do this, Matt just might be the guy.

"This might be what you say, but all I keep hearing are movie titles and such."

"I know, I know, but I've done my own research on it. Don't you see a movie then go and look up to see if it was real or not?"

Bryn thought to herself that she had done that before, but she could only imagine to what lengths he might have gone to.

"I played this game and it had—"

"Enough about the games. Will anything work at all? Is this temporary?"

"Um, no, an EMP fries everything, but like I said, I don't know for sure, but it certainly looks like it could've been a big blast."

"So what does this mean? The police will come by soon, right?"

"Unless they have different cars than we do, nope."

Bryn looked around. More people had come outside to look around and try to start their cars. She looked back at Matt, who stood looking at her like an eager puppy. "Well, isn't this some shit?"

Ten Miles North of San Felipe, Mexico

The waves from the Sea of Cortez's warm salty water ebbed and flowed over Michael's body, now half buried in the beach's sand.

His clothes were torn and singed. Scrapes, cuts and

bruises covered the skin that was exposed. His rugged face covered by a thick beard showed the signs of trauma as well; his nose was broken, lips scabbed, and his right eye was swollen shut, dark purple bruising extending out from it.

If someone were walking down the beach, they might have thought he was a dead man, but he wasn't. Killing Michael McNeil was something his enemies had tried, but once again he had narrowly escaped.

A larger wave crashed over him.

His left hand moved, fingers grasping at the sand. With all the effort he could muster, he pushed the weight of his large muscular frame onto his back. With a loud gasp he took in a breath. The one good eye opened but quickly closed as the bright morning light hurt.

"Argh!" he said out loud. Allowing his eye to adjust, he looked around the secluded beachhead but found nothing to his left or right but seagulls, sand crabs and endless beach.

A painful grimace gripped his face as he tried to get up. After a minute of struggling, he was sitting up.

More waves lapped his legs. The water was warm, but he would need to find new clothes or at least dry the ones he had on before nightfall.

He didn't recognize the beach and couldn't remember how he'd gotten there. He struggled to recall how he'd gotten on the beach and in the condition he was in, but nothing came to him.

Out just beyond the horizon, a large plume of smoke billowed from the waters. He wondered if he came from there. Was he on a boat? He pressed his one eye closed and placed his head between his legs and said, "Think, damn it, where are you?"

Nothing came.

He looked out towards the water again and the thick black smoke still hung in the sky. His gut instincts told him that smoke and his physical condition were connected, but how?

Knowing he couldn't survive on the beach, especially in his current state, he stood. A crooked grin stretched across his face when he discovered his legs could support him.

He was unsure which direction he should go. By the location of the sun, he guessed the beach ran north-south. In those directions he saw nothing but beach, with no signs of people or structures. To the west the wide beach ran into a steep cliff, but west was where he knew he needed to go if he were going to find help. Not knowing what body of water lay out there like an ocean or sea and with nothing to guide him, he decided to go north; no real reason, it was just a snap decision.

An hour of lumbering north didn't produce the results he had hoped for and needed. Tired, he looked for a shady place along the cliffs to take a break. His head throbbed, and upon an examination of the back of his head he found a large lump and cut buried beneath his thick brown hair. Running his fingers over the jagged cut, he had no doubt this wound was the cause of his memory loss.

The salty sea air blew harder as morning turned to afternoon. His mouth was parched and his stomach tightened and growled with hunger. A strong urge to lie down and sleep hit him, but he now feared he might have a concussion. Determined to find a safe place to care for his wounds, he got back to his feet and continued north.

The sun beat down on him. His thirst more than anything was becoming unbearable. How funny to be next to this large body of water but not be able to drink a drop. Fatigue was hindering his already slow pace, and when he looked down the beach he saw nothing. The cliff was lowering but nowhere was there a break in the sandstone to begin his climb west.

He stopped and looked all around him. The smoke he'd seen earlier was still there but farther south. He had covered some distance but not enough to lose sight of it. His body ached and a feeling of vertigo began to grip him.

He took a step, but upon going for a second, his legs gave out. He tumbled to the ground, his knees hitting first followed by his right arm then head. As he lay upon the warm sand, he searched for anything that might help him. Nothing came. Amnesia had stolen his memory and soon his fatigue, thirst and hunger would steal his consciousness. The darkness came quickly, but just before he closed his one eye, a voice called out in the distance.

USS *Harpers Ferry*, 125 Miles off the Coast of Southern California

"Marines, get off your asses; we have a formation on the flight deck, right now!" Gunny Roberts yelled into the berthing space.

"Roger that, Gunny," Vincent replied, swinging his legs out of the rack.

The Marines of Weapons Company, First Battalion, First Marine Regiment began to stir and grumble as they laced up their boots, buttoned their blouses and grabbed their covers.

Sergeant Gunner Vincent was the Marine's Marine; even his name portended his beloved career as a military man. Born and raised in the small mountain town of Challis, Idaho, he was a mountain man through and through, but even though he loved his snowcapped granite peaks, he couldn't wait to leave and sail the world. He knew he'd end up back in Idaho someday, but for now he believed his life belonged to the Marine Corps. He was tall, standing at an even six foot and his build was lean and mean. His esprit de corps was at ten on a scale of ten, but when it came to his hair, he couldn't do the high and tights. Maybe it was because of his father's premature baldness that he chose to have the bare minimum regulation haircut so as to preserve his sandy blond locks.

When he exited the hatch onto the flight deck, he noticed a sense of excitement not typical of a normal formation. He was running late and rushed to his spot within the ranks, barely making the call to attention.

Gunny Roberts called the unit to attention, turned and waited for the company commander, Captain Dupree, to approach.

Dupree marched over to Roberts, turned and stood. Roberts saluted and said, "Weapons Company all present and accounted for."

"Thank you, Gunny," Dupree said, offering his salute.

Roberts brought his salute back and marched off.

Looking out over the men all standing at attention, Dupree finished by yelling, "Weapons at ease!"

Dupree was a tall and sturdy-looking man. He had a hardened face, light eyes and thick, dark hair that he kept groomed with a flattop haircut. His stature coupled with his personality made him appear like a giant to some of the Marines. He looked out on the three hundred Marines in front of him. While Marine life was difficult for many, it came easy to Dupree. This occasion was different, though; to have to address the Marines about any situation back home was uncomfortable at best, especially since they were only days out from returning. The whole reason these Marines traveled so far from home was to defend their loved ones, but now he had to tell them that their homeland was threatened, their loved ones in harm's way, and they weren't there to protect them. "Marines, I am not going to stand here and bullshit you. You know me well enough to know I am a plain-spoken Marine. I tell it like it is. I never sugarcoat it," Dupree said as he began walking back and forth in front of the assembled Marines. "So I will tell you right now that our plans on returning home have changed and all leave that was planned has been cancelled!"

The Marines of Weapons Company all started looking to one another for clarification. Their overseas deployment was days from being over. The units that comprised the 11th Marine Expeditionary Unit were two days sail from pulling back into their home port of San Diego.

Dupree stopped his pacing to drop the real news. "Marines, initial reports suggest our country has suffered a massive attack. The intelligence we have received so far indicates that a nuclear weapon was detonated in the atmosphere above the Midwest."

Marines began to chatter and talk.

Roberts hollered out, "At ease, Marines!"

"At this time we have been given orders to steam back to Camp Pendleton. We'll disembark via the LCACs and assist the Marine units there," he said then paused. He looked out over his men with pride and continued. "Men, we've been through a lot together, we've fought together, we've bled together and some of us sacrificed all for God, country and Corps. This news of an attack on the homeland comes as a shock, and I know all of you must be thinking about family and loved ones back home. I'd be lying if I said I wasn't, too, but we have a new mission; we are United States Marines and we must not fail. Our country needs us now more than ever!" He stopped his pacing and again looked intently at his Marines, their stiff bodies swaying with the movement of the ship on the waves. He was proud of what his men had accomplished in their six-month deployment overseas, and he knew he would continue to be proud of them in this new mission.

Finished, he walked back to his position centered on the company, stood at attention and yelled, "Company, attention!"

Gunny Roberts walked around Dupree until he faced him, and then saluted.

Dupree saluted back and said, "Get these Marines prepared to disembark in two days."

"Yes, sir," Roberts replied.

Dupree cut his salute and walked away.

Loud chatter erupted the second the berthing door closed behind Vincent and his fellow Marines. A range of emotions was on display as some vented their anger by punching wall lockers, others yelled and some just sat in silence pondering what type of world they were heading into.

Vincent wasn't one to get emotionally worked up or charged. He went back to his rack, climbed in and closed the curtains. Dupree was right, he was one of the Marines who were very concerned about his family, but they were all the way up in Idaho.

A tap on his rack jolted him from his worried thoughts. "Yes, what is it?"

"Sergeant Vincent, it's Berg."

"What is it?"

"I just came from the CIC, and you gotta hear what they're saying," Lance Corporal Berg said, the tone of his voice showing a glimmer of excitement. Something that Vincent found disgusting.

Vincent pulled the drapes aside and asked, "What's the scoop?"

"So the intel coming in says a nuclear weapon was blown up in the atmosphere, and you know what happens when that sort of thing occurs, right?"

"Yes, an electromagnetic pulse. I know this, you know this, we all know this."

"Yeah, yeah, but the initial reports they're receiving is nothing is working, I mean nothing. In fact, even a lot of the equipment—Humvees, MRAPs, cars, trucks, you name it—at Pendleton is down."

"I don't get your point?"

"The point is a conventional EMP shouldn't do that. You remember from our NBC classes at SOI, EMPs aren't universal in their effects and the range can be limited."

"Get to the point, Berg, would you?"

"I heard them say this was a super-EMP, a weapon designed to inflict widespread and universal damage. Dude, the grid is down coast-to-coast, no cars are working, the world has come to a fucking halt. It's crazy train back home."

"Why am I getting a sense you're a bit too happy?"

"I'm not, but I am too. It's almost as good as a zombie apocalypse. This shit is crazy."

"If that's it, I want to get some shut-eye," Vincent said and closed the drapes.

"Are we getting chow together in a couple hours?" Berg asked.

"Sure, now leave me alone," Vincent pleaded. His mind drifted back to his family. He could see his mother doing what she does best, but his father, he could see him getting very upset by this.

How could this sort of thing have occurred? He thought to himself. How was it possible to pull this off? Confusion led to anger, which transformed into concern for his family. He had joined the Marine Corps to keep the country safe and secure by fighting their enemies overseas and thousands of miles away from home, but that had changed. The bastards, he thought, had pulled off an attack that had crippled his beloved country and put his family in direct jeopardy, but he was unable to go help them. How could this be? He stopped asking the questions because it didn't matter, it had happened. What he needed to focus on was his new mission, but more selfishly, he needed to find a way to check on his family. Just how he'd do that was still unknown.

Carlsbad, CA

Nicholas grunted as he pulled the manual cord to disengage the electronic garage door and pushed it up. Light poured into the windowless garage.

"I'm here. What do you want to show me?" Becky asked.

"Where's Abby?" he asked.

"Getting ready for school."

He climbed into their Mercedes GL450 SUV and hit the ignition button. Nothing happened. "Um, I don't think we're going anywhere. The car won't start." He dug in his pocket to ensure he had the smart key on him; it was there and he tried again. Nothing.

"Really?" Becky asked, astonished.

Abigail appeared, dressed head to toe like a defiant teenager, wearing tight jeans and a low-cut top. "Take your time, Dad. I don't need to go to school today," Abigail said with a snarky grin stretched across her face and her phone in her hands. She was still relentlessly trying to get it to work.

"Your dad's right. You're not going anywhere, and it's not because of the car. Go back upstairs and change your clothes," Becky snapped.

"Whatever, Mom," Abigail replied, then mouthed what Becky had just said.

"What was that?" Becky asked Abigail.

"Nothing," Abigail answered, walking back into the house.

The blood ran out of Nicholas' face as his deep-seated concern turned to fear. He stepped out of the car, exited the garage, and quickly walked down the driveway towards the street.

"Where are you going?" Becky asked as she followed him out, her bathrobe flowing.

Nicholas didn't answer. He reached the street and looked towards the main road in the distance. Their house was perched atop a hill and had a three-hundred-and-sixty-degree view, including the road that fed into Rancho Del Sur.

"What are you looking at?" Becky asked, now standing

beside him.

"Do me a favor. In the second drawer there's a set of binoculars; get those for me," he said.

"Binoculars? What are you trying to look at?" Becky asked.

"Never mind, I'll do it myself." He marched off. A moment later he came back with the small black binoculars. He put them to his eyes, adjusted the focus and looked at the road. Just as he assumed, no cars were moving. What vehicles he did see were stopped and people were milling around them.

"Nic, what's going on?" Becky asked, now concerned.

"I don't know, but I want to see if the cars I saw earlier are still at the entrance," he answered.

Becky looked at him, concern written on her face. "You're scaring me."

"Look," he said, handing her the binoculars. "Look at Poinsettia Road, tell me what you see."

Nervously she took the binoculars and looked where he told her. "I see cars stopped in the road and people walking around."

"Here, give them to me," he said.

She handed them over. He briskly walked around to the back of the house. He again put the binoculars to his eyes and said, "Fuck me."

She hustled up behind him and asked, "Same thing?"

"Yep, I-5 is dead. Nothing is moving. It looks like a traffic jam, but nothing is moving. I don't see any lights, nothing."

"What's going on?"

"I don't know."

"Is it some kind of terrorist attack?"

"You tell me. Nothing works, our car won't start, our phones won't work, the power is out and every car I see isn't working."

They both just stared into the distance. He wanted to give her an answer to what might be happening, but he didn't really know for sure. His old Marine Corps training gave him some clues and his most recent training with prepper groups had given him greater insight, but seeing it all now seemed so surreal. The world that man had built had come to a halt, but Mother Nature didn't. The waves of the ocean still crashed against the beach, the cool sea air still blew, the clouds still raced across the sky, and the animals continued upon their daily routines.

"This is a terrorist attack, it has to be," Nicholas said.

"Should we contact someone?"

He turned and looked at her. "With what, cups and a string?"

"You don't have to be an ass."

"I'm sorry, but I knew something bad would happen one day and it's here."

"Nick, it's not that I never believed you, it's just—"

"So all of the eye rolling every time I bought more guns or food or took classes, that wasn't saying something?"

"Let's not get worked up. We don't know how big this is," Becky said, trying to convince him but mostly trying to reassure herself that the situation wasn't as bad as he might now think it was.

"Are you trying to convince me or yourself that this isn't a big deal?"

"I need to check on my parents."

"One thing at a time," he said. He headed back to the garage and looked at both their cars. He jumped into the second vehicle, a BMW 3 Series, but like the Mercedes, it was dead.

Frustrated, he leaned his forehead against the steering wheel and muttered, "Idiot."

"Should we be doing something?" Becky asked, now standing next to the car.

The question was exactly what he needed to hear. He was a man of purpose and having something to focus on was critical to his mental stability. The walls of the garage showed months of preparedness. One shelving unit after another was filled with large plastic containers of freeze-dried or dehydrated foods, fifty cases of bottled water and large plastic bins with camping gear, backpacks, clothing, boots, and seemingly endless smaller items he had acquired for his family's survival. The one thing that was missing was a vehicle that worked.

"Nic, are you listening to me?" Becky asked.

He was lost in thought but came back when she touched his shoulder. "Nic?"

"We need more water."

"Where are we going to get more bottled water?"

"Not bottled, from our taps."

"I'm not drinking tap water," she replied, her face cringing.

"You'll bathe in it, but God forbid you have to drink

it? Go get Abby, start filling all the tubs and sinks, then fill every container we have with tap water. We have a solid supply of drinking water here, but we can use tap water for cleaning and hygiene. Let's conserve it now," he said, getting out of the car and rushing inside.

She followed him inside and to the kitchen.

He immediately went to work by filling his first glass and placing it on the counter.

She took his lead and began to fill glasses too.

Abigail came into the kitchen and blurted out, "What the hell are you doing?"

"Start filling glasses, anything you can find," Nicholas ordered.

"O-M-G, my parents have lost their minds," Abigail joked.

Becky stopped what she was doing and got in her face. "Enough attitude. There's been some sort of terrorist attack. No more smart-ass comments. Go and fill all the tubs."

Abigail raised her eyebrows and her mouth hung open in astonishment. "Fine," she replied and stomped off.

"That girl is so sassy!" Becky said.

"Like mother like daughter," Nicholas cracked.

"Don't put that on me. She looks like you and acts like you."

A loud banging on the front door halted their back and forth.

"I'll get it," Nicholas said and bolted out of the kitchen.

He couldn't think who might be there but suspected a

neighbor. A glimpse through the peephole confirmed it was his neighbor Brent.

Nicholas unlocked the heavy alder door and opened it.

"Hi, sorry to bother you," Brent said sheepishly.

"Hey, Brent, what can I help you with?" Nicholas asked, deliberately not inviting him in.

Brent, his wife, Evelyn, and young child, Toby, had moved next to them two years before. Becky welcomed them to the neighborhood by having them over for a dinner party and then two weeks later invited them to a small gathering of other friends so they could meet some new people. They had moved to San Diego from Washington State for Brent's work and knew only a few people. That last party was the final time they had socially hung out. Several weeks after, Brent had a party and never invited them; this happened several more times after that. Not a year later, Brent had reported Nicholas to the HOA board, complaining of too much noise during a party. Nicholas never forgave them for the snubs, but the formal complaint put Nicholas over the top; he could never look at Brent again without having the urge to tell him off.

"I was wondering if your power is working." Brent asked.

Just looking at Brent's short stature and thinning black hair repulsed Nicholas. "No power here either."

"What about your car?"

"No."

Brent could feel the negative energy between them but was relentless in his questioning. "Um, any chance you might know someone who has a car?"

"No."

"You sure?"

Nicholas exhaled deeply and asked, "What do you need?"

"Toby needs medicine. His inhaler will be running out soon, and we need to pick up his refills."

"Sorry, I can't help you."

"Hi, Brent, how's Evelyn?" Becky asked, walking up behind Nicholas.

"Oh, hi, Becky, um, she's fine. We're just worried about this outage; it's so strange."

"Is that it?" Nicholas asked bluntly. If a stare could move people, Nicholas' deep gaze would have thrown Brent ten feet from the door.

"Yeah, but if you hear about someone who has a car, please let me know."

"Sure, will do," Nicholas said and closed the door.

Becky smacked his shoulder and said, "Did you have to be so rude?"

"As a matter of fact, yes, I did, but I will have to thank him. His questions about a car jogged my memory."

"Glad to see you can find the positives in things," Becky said and headed back to the kitchen.

"Don't you want to hear what it is?"

"I don't need to ask. I've known you for eighteen years; I know you're going to tell me."

He stepped into the kitchen and grabbed her tightly; her spiritedness often turned him on.

She pulled away and said, "No, not going to happen."

"Then I'll be on my way."

"Where to?"

"Your parents' house."

"My parents, that'll take you an hour or more walking."

"It'll take me thirty minutes on my mountain bike, but if my hunch is right, it'll only take me ten minutes to drive home."

"What?"

"Your dad has that old Dodge Dart in his spare garage space. I think whatever has happened seems to have destroyed sensitive circuitry, and that old 1963 Dart doesn't have anything like that. I'm willing to wager, and you know I'm not a betting man, that his old car will work."

San Diego, CA

With the best explanation for the outage given to her, Bryn decided she better start looking towards getting supplies, as she had exactly nothing. Not one to have enough food to get her through a week, she was a bit freaked out by the possibility of what she was told. If nothing ever worked again, what did that mean? The concept seemed so foreign. She had never given something like this a thought, not even a little bit. Like most people, she went about her life living day to day, only thinking ahead enough to schedule her next outing with friends.

"We're going to need more food," Bryn said, looking at the three cans of Campbell's tomato soup, half-eaten box of Wheat Thins, four packages of ramen noodles, and assorted bags of potato and tortilla chips. Her refrigerator was no better.

Sophie held it open, looking for something to eat. "I'm so hungry, but nothing looks good."

Bryn, upset by not having anything, looked at Sophie. "Hey, don't stand there with the door open. You're letting out the cool air."

Sophie shut it and snottily said, "There's nothing in there anyway. Let's go to the store and get some stuff, then."

"We're going to have to. Come on, let's go," Bryn said, grabbing her jacket.

Sophie was right behind her, hoodie in hand to keep her warm against the cool December late afternoon. She was an inch taller than her older sister, almost five foot seven inches, with shoulder-length brown hair, which was thick and typically pulled back. She kept her natural color as compared to Bryn, who dyed her hair blonde. While proclaiming she wasn't a victim to style or fashion, she followed the tight-knit regime of the supposed revolt against it. Most of her clothes were vintage, all purchased from consignment or Salvation Army stores, makeup was kept at a minimum, and her hair kept as natural as possible. Bryn didn't care much for this look, but she was happy that Sophie hadn't gone over the edge and begun wearing patchouli.

"So where should we go?" Sophie asked.

"There's a grocery store down the street," she answered as they were walking down the stairs outside her apartment.

At the bottom were several men, twenty-something, smoking and laughing.

"Where you off to, Bryn?" one man, Latino looking, asked.

"To the store."

"Cool, can you grab me a pack of smokes?" another white man asked. He dug into his pocket and pulled out some cash.

Bryn passed them, turned, and the cash in the man's hand got her attention. She suddenly realized that she didn't have a lot of money and that with the power down, she wouldn't be able to use her credit card.

Sophie walked between the men and grabbed his cash and asked, "What kind?"

"Marlboro Reds. So, what's your name again?" the white man asked.

"I'm Sophie, you?"

"Dylan."

"I'm Alberto," the Latino man said.

"Hey, Alberto," Sophie said with a flirtatious tone.

"And I'm Craig," the third guy said.

Bryn brushed by them all and ran back up to her apartment to get what cash she had hidden. She dashed inside, opened her jewelry box and pulled out a small stack of bills. She counted it, and to her dismay, it came to only three hundred and fifty-three. That would get her somewhere, but she knew not far enough. Not wanting to waste time, she raced back out. When she hit the stairs, she saw Sophie smoking, but it wasn't a cigarette.

"Seriously?" she blurted out.

"You go ahead. I'm going to hang here," Sophie said, then took another hit off the joint.

"Not happening," Bryn said as she grabbed Sophie by her arm and pulled her up.

"Hey, I'm just having a bit of fun."

"Come on, Bryn, she just wants to party," Alberto barked.

"Not now she doesn't," Bryn shot back at him.

All three men began to chide Bryn as she walked away grumbling something unintelligible.

"I love you, sis, but you can be a real pain in my ass," Sophie said.

"I was thinking the same thing."

"Why are you being so…irritating?"

"I'm not."

"Then why the rush to go to the store? You're on edge. This is cool. Finally the system is down. Now maybe we can get back to the way humans were supposed to be. I kinda dig it. Look, people are out talking and kids are playing, riding their bikes instead of having their heads in an iPad."

"This isn't normal. I went through the blackout a few years ago; that was cool. This is different; something else is going on. The cars don't work, fuck, nothing works."

They were now on the main sidewalk along Genesee Avenue. There they saw the results of the outage. Cars lying still, left by their occupants' hours ago after they realized they weren't going to start and no one was coming to help them. Many had their hoods up and trunks open. People were milling around outdoors and the sounds of talking, yelling, and laughter echoed from the small apartment complex. Both Bryn and Sophie were looking around in wonderment at it all, their senses taking in everything in front of them, and they didn't hear the patter of feet behind them until it was right on top of them.

Bryn spun around, ready to fight, a small canister of pepper spray held out.

"Whoa!" Matt called out, holding his hands up. He had stopped in his tracks upon seeing the pepper spray.

"You scared the shit out of us!" Bryn exclaimed.

"Sorry, I saw you guys leaving and I thought I'd tag along."

"Sure," Bryn said, as she turned and began to walk again.

They talked about the outage and the possibility of it being what Matt thought it was. Sophie continued to expose her belief that it was a good thing to destroy the overly materialistic and self-absorbed society so that a balance could be reestablished.

Bryn thought her sister was naïve and openly stated it.

"When did you become such a goddamn hippie?" Bryn asked.

"What?"

"Yeah, you're the perfect example of the pampered and clueless generation that wants everything that gave you safety and all the comforts that you enjoy to just go away. It's foolish and stupid."

"Foolish and stupid? This coming from the princess who cares about her looks and her perfect blonde hair."

"I care about how I look. I don't go out of my way to make a statement about looks then make sure I have a specific look. So much talk about judgment from your type and all you do is judge," Bryn shot back.

"You know, if this is what I have to deal with, I'll just go back and party with those guys. I don't need this shit."

Bryn stopped and grabbed Sophie. Matt kept his mouth shut and observed the siblings' fight in fascination.

"I love you, but I need you to wake the fuck up. This isn't right and what you think is so cool can become fucking really bad."

"You're such a stress monster, always have been," Sophie responded as she jerked her arm away and continued to walk.

Bryn jogged up to her and again stopped her. "Let's agree to this. I'll stop talking, you stop talking, and let's get some groceries and go home."

Sophie looked at her and nodded in agreement.

Matt came jogging up and said, "Hey, guys, this doesn't look good."

All turned their attention to the mob and violent activity occurring at the grocery store a hundred yards ahead of them.

Bryn and Sophie had been so enthralled with their petty fight they didn't notice what was going on around them.

"What the fuck is going on?" Bryn asked.

"Looks like everyone else had the same idea we had," Matt said.

"Is this what happens in all your sci-fi movies?"

"Yeah, pretty much," Matt answered.

"What should we do?" Sophie asked, a tinge of fear in her voice as she watched people running around. Screams and yelling now filled their ears.

"We have to eat. Let's go," Bryn said and began to march towards the chaos.

The closer they got to the parking lot of Vons supermarket, the greater the chaos came into sharp relief. People were dashing in and out of the smashed glass doors along the store frontage. Yelling and cries of panic filled the open air as they drew closer and closer.

An elderly woman came rushing out of the store with a half-full cart when two teenage boys ran over to her. One punched her in the face while the other grabbed the cart. The teen thugs had been waiting for the opportunity to prey upon someone and knew the woman was an easy target. The woman cried out after being punched in the face, stumbled and fell to the hard pavement. With a look of terror on her face, she reached out in vain to stop her attackers, but her small attempt was no match for the young men. Both teens were laughing as they charged ahead in Bryn's direction with the cart of food.

Seeing this enraged Bryn. As if on autopilot she ran up to them and said, "Hey, douche bags!" She leveled her pepper spray at one and pressed the button. A long stream burst out, hitting the teen pushing the cart in the face. Screaming out in pain, he let go of the cart and began to wipe his eyes frantically. The second teen, seeing his friend hurt and Bryn turning towards him ran off, leaving his friend behind. Bryn walked up to the teen still crying out in pain, and kicked him in the crotch as she screamed, "Fucking piece of shit!"

The teen howled in pain as he crumpled to the ground.

Just for good measure, she pointed the spray and hit him again.

Sophie and Matt came running up behind her, shocked at her prowess and fearless engagement of the two teens.

"Holy shit, Bryn that was badass!" Sophie bellowed with pride.

Bryn ignored her and jogged over to the elderly woman and helped her up. "You okay?"

"Thank you, thank you."

As Bryn was showing charity to this woman, people still came pouring out of the store, pushing carts or carrying what they could in their arms.

"Bring her cart over!" Bryn ordered Matt.

He briskly walked over and gave it to her. "Here."

The woman took it and said, "God bless you!"

Bryn cracked a slight smile, turned to Sophie and Matt and said, "Let's go shopping."

San Felipe, Mexico

"No, no, no!" Michael screamed, and then opened his one good eye. He blinked repeatedly, and when his vision focused, he found that he was no longer on the beach. He was in a darkened room, lying on a bed. This alarmed him. He sat up, but the pain suddenly reminded him of his wounds.

Something scurried to his right.

"Who's that?" he asked.

A giggle was the only response.

"Who is that?"

Again a giggle was the answer.

"Hey, come here, please." Michael beckoned from the bed, knowing there was a small child there.

A small black-haired girl poked her head from behind a chair in the corner. She giggled loudly and resumed hiding.

"Little girl, please talk to me. Where am I?"

"*Maria, donde estas?*" a voice blared out from the other room. Soon the bedroom door opened and there stood the source of the voice, a short and burly man.

"Maria, no!"

The little girl squealed and ran out of the room.

"Mister, please help me. Where am I?"

"You're awake, I see, *bueno*," the man said.

Michael could barely make out the almost black silhouette of the man. The light from behind the man hid his finer features.

"Did you find me?" Michael asked.

"No, my son did. You were not in good shape, my friend," the man answered with a thick accent.

Michael looked around the sparsely lit room. "Where am I?"

"My house, *senor.*"

"Where, though, what city?"

"San Felipe."

"United States?"

"Ha, no, *senor*, you're in Mexico."

Michael grimaced when a sharp pain rose from the back of his head. He lay back down and rested his head in the feather-down pillow.

"My wife cleaned your wounds. Are you in some type of trouble?"

"Did you contact the police?"

"No *policia*, my friend, you're safe here."

"Why?"

"You look like a nice man, no need to involve the *federales* or local *policia*. Let's say I don't want to see them either."

Michael nodded. "*Gracias* for your help."

"Are you hungry?" the man asked.

"Yeah, I'm starving."

"I hope you like tacos de cabeza."

"Sure, anything sounds good."

"What's your name, *senor*?"

Michael had to think for second, but it came to him. "Michael."

"*Mucho gusto*, Michael, my name is Jose. Welcome to my *casa*."

"Thank you, Jose."

"I'll be back with some food," Jose said and closed the door, leaving Michael in the darkened room.

The only light present in the room came through a slit in the blinds. It cast a long beam of light on the wall and illuminated a crucifix.

Michael stared at the cross with the crucified body of Jesus on it. A feeling that he'd been blessed in this particular situation came over him. He wasn't a deeply religious man that he could remember, but having Jose and his family find him seemed perfect. Not knowing why he was on the beach and where he suffered his wounds led him to believe that he might not be a good guy, so to speak. If the police had found him, he'd probably be in jail, and Mexican jails weren't the luxury accommodations their American counterparts were.

Knowing his name was a victory for him. He went through the database that was his mind, and hazy images of being in uniform flashed as did a man who looked like him. He couldn't recall his name, but the man he saw must be his brother.

A tap on the door jolted him.

The door opened, and there stood Jose holding a small tray. He walked in and set it on the nightstand.

Michael sat up while Jose stuffed more pillows behind him.

"Here you go, tacos de cabeza, one of my wife's specialties."

"Looks delicious, thank you," Michael said. The plate held three small tacos, a side of refried beans and rice. It looked like typical Mexican fare.

Jose pulled the blinds back.

Light splashed across the room.

Not paying attention to the room and its contents, Michael was eating ferociously.

A giggle from the doorway pulled him away from his food. He saw the little girl again and waved. "Hola."

She giggled and hid.

"Sorry about my little Maria, she's not accustomed to seeing Americans. You are American, right?"

"Ha, I think I am," Michael answered while he pointed at his head. "I don't know for sure. I can't remember much."

"I'll let you eat, enjoy."

"This is so good. What is cabeza?"

Jose hesitated but finally said, "Cow."

"Hmm, it's so good. Tell your wife thank you and that she's an excellent cook."

"I will, Michael."

Jose left but just before he closed the door, Maria shouted, "Cabeza is cow head!"

Michael stopped chewing and looked in between the freshly made corn tortillas. He shrugged his shoulders and continued to devour them.

Finishing the entire plate of food, Michael felt satiated and happy. Resting back into the thick pillows, he tried to piece together what he might be doing in San Felipe, Mexico, and what he might have been doing offshore in the Sea of Cortez. Nothing came to him as he searched the fragmented images in his mind. It would help if he knew what he did for a living, but all he could see was a younger him in a camouflage uniform. Maybe he was still in the service, and if so, what was he doing in Mexico. None of it made sense.

A loud tap and the doorknob turned.

Michael sat up ready for Jose to return so he could ask

him some questions.

The door opened, but it wasn't Jose. A tall man stood there with two others behind him.

A quick glance told Michael they weren't very nice. He adjusted in the bed and looked for something he might use to protect himself.

The men came into the room but not towards him. They surrounded the bed and hovered over him. A fourth man walked in, pulled up a small chair and sat down.

"Michael, hello," the man said.

"Who are you?"

"That's of no concern to you; I'm more concerned about you."

Michael felt nervous; his eyes darted around the room to each man. Though they didn't openly carry any weapons, he had no doubt the men were armed.

"What are you doing in San Felipe?" the man asked.

Michael turned his attention back to him. He was a tall man, lean and handsome. His jet black hair was slicked back and his face was cleanly shaven. His dark brown eyes were hidden below thick black eyebrows. His dress was semiformal with freshly ironed black slacks and a linen shirt worn under a camel-hair sports jacket.

"I can't remember much. As you can see, I'm a bit busted up."

"Yes, I see you're not doing well. How did you come to receive those injuries?"

"I don't know."

"How did you come to be on the beach?"

"I don't know."

The man looked at one of his colleagues and nodded. The large man walked over to Michael and grabbed his left arm.

Michael pulled away but not quick enough.

The man grabbed it again and twisted it into an arm bar.

Michael screamed out in pain.

"Now, why are you in San Felipe?"

Seething in pain, Michael answered, "I don't know.'

The large man twisted his arm farther.

"Ahhh, damn it, that hurts. I don't know, I swear. I got hit in the head. I don't remember anything."

"Do you know anything about the missile launch last night?"

"What missile? I don't know anything."

The man leaned in close to Michael's face and said, "You end up on our beach injured. A ship that apparently launched a large missile or rocket is now smoldering out at sea and you don't know anything? Ask me why I should believe you."

Michael begged, "Please let me go and I'll tell you what you want to hear."

The man looked up and nodded.

The large man released his arm and stepped back.

Michael rubbed his arm and said, "I must have been on that ship you're speaking of, but I don't remember anything. I believe my memory is coming back, and when it does, you'll be the first person I tell."

The man looked at the large man, who stepped forward again.

"No, don't, please. Look, see my head, see this bandage. I got hit with something big. I have amnesia. Look at me, I'm injured badly. I'm not going anywhere. Let me stay, heal up, and as soon as I remember, I'll tell you."

"Wait," the man said to the large man. "Marco, you'll stay here, keep an eye on our American friend. Let us know when he remembers."

"Are you police or something?" Michael asked.

"No, just concerned citizens."

"What do you care about a ship or missile?"

"We care because whatever was shot from that ship destroyed our electrical grid and everything else."

Like a light bulb had gone off in his head, Michael remembered something. An image of the ship popped in his head along with the missile on a large pad. He hoped his newfound recollection wasn't given away. He needed to figure out how to escape before he could tell them anything. What he saw was his value as a captive going to zero upon his full disclosure.

"The grid is down?" Michael asked.

"Yes, and everything else. Nothing electrical works, including most cars, and I have no doubt it was because of that missile."

"I still don't know what you care, if you're not the cops."

"Because you're valuable if you know something, even to the cops. I can get a lot of money for you," the man said and stood. Looking at Marco, he said, "Don't let our friend go anywhere, understand?"

"Yes, sir."

The man and the others left.

Michael could hear them talking behind the door. Soon their voices became silent.

The door opened again and Jose was there. "*Senor*, I'm so sorry, please forgive me. Manuel, the tall gentleman, is my employer. I mentioned something to one of his men, and they just showed up. I didn't tell them on purpose, you must believe me."

"Don't worry about it, Jose. Can you answer a couple questions for me?" Michael asked.

"*Si*, yes, of course," Jose said, stepping all the way into the room and taking a seat in the same chair where Manuel had just been.

"He mentioned the grid is down. Is there any other information about it, why or how?"

"No, sir, the electricity went out very early this morning, hasn't come back on."

"Did you see this missile launch?"

"*Si*, I did. I was working very early this morning and saw it. The rocket lit up the sky like it was daytime. Then not three minutes later a large explosion followed. It must have been the ship."

"Where was the missile going? I mean headed, what direction?"

"North, northeast."

"Okay, thanks. Oh, do your cars work? He said something about cars not working."

"Oh yes, my Datsun runs great. It's what I brought you home in."

"Thanks, Jose, sorry for the trouble. Let the big guy

know I'll be taking a nap. Hopefully I'll remember something."

Jose leaned in and said, "Don't remember too fast, okay?"

"Got it, understood."

"Get some rest," Jose said and left the bedroom.

When the door latched closed, Michael began to put some of the pieces together. He now remembered that he was on the ship and there was a missile. He also remembered fighting people, but he was hurt and then there was an explosion.

One tiny remnant of his memory came back slowly as he lay there. With is one good eye closed, he viewed the images that imprinted on his mind. Suddenly a name came that hadn't before, Nicholas. Was Nicholas someone he knew? Was it his brother, as he wanted to associate the name with the face of the younger man who looked similar to him? Another name followed right behind it, San Diego. Did Nicholas live in San Diego? Why was he having the name of that city enter his mind? Was he from San Diego?

Michael didn't know who exactly he was dealing with, but by their modus operandi, he knew they had to be cartel. That meant he would most certainly be killed once he told them what he knew. He had to get out of there as quickly as possible, but to where? Where would he go? Then he said under his breath, "San Diego."

Carlsbad, CA

Nicholas held the Sig Sauer P239 in his hand. He loved the feel, size and weight of this compact semi-auto pistol. He had grown up around firearms, but his father, a former highway patrolman, had loved his 'wheel guns', and if he had to carry a semi-auto, he went for the old reliable 1911. His older brother, Michael, had turned him on to Sigs. It took one time at the range with one and he was hooked. The safe that was hidden behind a false wall in his office closet held several models of Sigs, but besides his P220, the P239 was by far his absolute favorite. He holstered the pistol and zipped up a light jacket to conceal it.

On his way out of the office, he caught his reflection in the mirror and stopped. He looked at himself and pivoted back and forth to see if the pistol bulged from his jacket. The last thing he needed was to run into law enforcement and go to jail for carrying without a permit. However, he was willing to take the risk. He liked the old saying, 'Better to be tried by twelve than carried by six.'

As he continued to look at his reflection, he found it so odd that something had finally happened to warrant him carrying a concealed weapon. He liked the way he looked but oddly liked the excitement of what was happening. He was sure that would wane if things truly went bad, but for now he felt vindicated and relatively safe. Taking one last look, he bolted out of the office and right into Abigail.

"Dad, I was just coming to see you," Abigail said.

"What is it?"

"I want to come with you."

He placed his hands on her shoulders and said, "Not a good idea. Let me see what's happening out there first."

"That's why I should come; I can help you."

He smiled at her and gave her a kiss on the forehead. "I'll be fine. I'm just going to Nana's and Papa's. I'll take surface roads, and I doubt anything really bad is happening right now."

"But you think things will get bad?"

He had always protected her, and maintaining her innocence of the world had been a priority for him for so long, but she was sixteen, and if this got bad, he needed to make sure she had all the information she needed. "It could get bad. People don't handle power outages too well; history is our teacher in that regard."

She gave him a hug and felt the pistol. "You are worried."

"Just a precaution."

"Can I have one?"

He looked into her eyes and without reservation said, "Yes, but not now. When I get back, I'll set you up."

"But what if something happens while you're gone?"

"Nothing will. Keep the doors locked and you'll be fine. People are just coming to grips with this now. We'll need to be concerned when they realize they're screwed and the government isn't coming to save them."

Hearing them talk, Becky walked in from the kitchen. "Set her up with what?"

"Nothing," he replied. Getting into an argument about arming his sixteen-year-old was something he didn't need right now.

"Tell them they need to come back here," Becky insisted about her parents. She was worried about how they would be able to manage the situation.

"I can't guarantee that will happen."

"Maybe I should go with you," Becky said.

"No, stay here. I won't be gone that long."

"What else should we be doing?" Becky asked.

"Pack one of the backpacks I put in the bedroom. Only pack things you'll need, so high heels and cocktail dresses don't fall into that category."

She cut her eyes at him.

"I'm serious," he said.

"I'm not an idiot," she replied.

"I wasn't saying that, it's just..."

"What?"

Now was not a time to be petty, so he stopped short of saying anything. "Nothing, just put things together." He gave them both a kiss and left.

If his guide to what was happening in the world came from what he observed while he rode his bike through the streets of Rancho Del Sur, he would think nothing had happened. The people he did see were going about their day with no apparent concern. Many cars he saw had their hoods up while people were walking the sidewalks, talking, laughing and seemingly not overly concerned. Children were riding their bikes and playing outside. A sight he hadn't seen in many years.

Right now a normalcy bias ran through many people. Without a reasonable explanation, what had happened today was just another in a string of endless attacks that had been plaguing the country. It started several months ago with a few lone-wolf attacks on malls; men walking in, shouting, '*Allah Akbar!*' and then shooting. Also a few of the major cities had car bombs detonated at large events. San Diego had been lucky, but even there; those attacks had numbed many people. After the buzz of an attack wore off they went back to the malls, to schools, sporting events, etc. What were they to do, give up? Nicholas didn't think they should put their arms in the air and surrender, but at least people should ready themselves for the big one, and this he now thought must have been it.

Once outside the gates, a different picture began to emerge. Abandoned cars sat everywhere on the road. As he passed the first strip mall that housed an AM/PM convenient store, the realities of his future began to come into stark relief. A couple cars sat at the gas pumps, abandoned, but the storefront was smashed; people came out cradling food in their arms. In some ways he was surprised, he had this image of rioting and chaos exploding within hours, but couldn't imagine why someone would begin to loot. Did they know something he didn't? Were they sizing up the situation and thought they couldn't get caught?

Fortunately for him, the ride to his in-laws was mostly downhill. He prayed Frank would allow him to take the car, but he'd understand if he didn't. Why would he give up what might be one of the few operational vehicles in the area?

He made the left into the condo complex where his in-laws lived and again saw nothing unusual or out of sorts. Running Cedars was a retirement community that spanned five acres of beautifully manicured landscaping. The streets weaved around three dozen two-story condominium buildings, each housing four units each. The backs of the buildings faced an expansive common area with swimming pool, hot tub, horseshoe pits, barbeques and a large clubhouse. His in-laws loved living here, and he could see why, they needed for nothing.

A few people were out walking their dogs and taking in the typical sunny and bluebird San Diego day. They waved as he rode by, with no care in the world.

Outside their building, he stopped and hustled over to the front door, bike slung over his shoulder. The last thing he needed was to have someone steal his bike. Instinctually he hit the doorbell but couldn't hear it. He laughed to himself that he too had some actions tied to a world with electricity. After a few knocks on the door, it opened.

"Nicholas, what are you doing here?" Marjory, his mother-in-law, asked, surprised to see him.

"Hi, Mom, we've been calling, but with the power out, Becky thought it best I come over to see if you needed anything."

"Come in, come in," she said and stepped aside.

Nicholas stepped into the foyer. He marveled at how much natural light their little condo got. His mother-in-law had always been partial to homes with lots of windows, she couldn't stand a dark house, and fortunately for them she had that taste.

He liked his mother-in-law; she was sweet, generous

and engaging. He was never at a loss for words with her around, as she was a great conversationalist and never judged. However, when it came to the other half of his in-laws, it was the opposite. Frank was stiff, stubborn and very opinionated to the point of being righteous. Their relationship had struggled from the beginning after he overheard Frank telling Becky not to marry him because he wasn't going to amount to anything. Frank had later apologized, but it took years and proof that he did amount to something. That apology rang hollow to Nicholas and it strained what could have been something that Nicholas had wanted again, a father figure.

Nicholas only had his older brother for family, as both of their parents were dead. Their father had died from a heart attack when Nicholas was ten, and his mother lost her fight to breast cancer eight years after. Nicholas felt lost after his mother's death and followed in his brother's footsteps by joining the military, but unlike his brother who went into the army and became a Ranger, he joined the Marines. From the Marines he went to college, but he found college boring. He wanted more, and to him college was a job machine. He floated from job to job until an old friend told him to pursue being a stock broker. That was it for him; he started working for a small firm and eventually owned his own.

"Do you guys need anything?" Nicholas asked.

"Can you believe this power outage? You'll have to excuse me, but I think it's fun. Frank, on the other hand, is not too happy. He's been seething that he can't call the electric company."

"I think something worse than a typical power outage has occurred."

"Can I get you something to drink?" she asked.

"Um, no, I'm good," he replied, following her into the kitchen.

From the back den, Frank's hollering came through the thin walls.

"Frank, stop trying to call SDG&E and come say hi to Nicholas," Marjory called out.

"Who?" Frank asked.

"Nicholas is here."

"One second."

"Listen, I think you guys should come home with me. It will be more comfortable for you two. I have plenty of food," Nicholas offered.

"We're not going anywhere," Frank bellowed as he came into the room. He brushed his thin gray hair to the side with his fingers then tucked his bright green polo shirt into his khaki pants.

Nicholas and Becky had a running joke that her father must own stock in Izod as he had five of each color of polo shirt.

Frank walked past Nicholas and opened the refrigerator and took out a jug of orange juice.

Nicholas took notice of how loose fitting the khakis were on him.

"Can I make you some lunch?" Marjory asked them.

"Mom, I'm fine. I need to talk to you about what's going on," Nicholas stressed, raising his voice slightly.

"Don't tell me, this power outage is the end of the

world?" Frank quipped then took a drink of his orange juice.

"You haven't been outside, have you?" Nicholas lamented.

"If you came over here to spread your doomsday scenarios, please spare me," Frank said, scolding him.

That comment made Nicholas want to walk out; he had lost patience with people's attitudes a long time ago. "Dad, this is more than a power outage. Cars aren't working; my mobile phone and other electronics are dead."

"Oh dear," Marjory said.

Frank clenched his jaw and said, "I'm sure the president is handling the situation. The power will be back up soon enough. You just gotta have patience. I swear you and the younger generations can't sit still."

"That may be, but Becky wants you two to come home with me. She's worried about you."

"Maybe we should," Marjory said, looking at Frank.

Frank cut a look at her and then put his attention back on Nicholas. "We'll be fine. There's no need to be an alarmist about these things."

"I'm not being an alarmist; something isn't right."

"Listen, son, my parents lived through Pearl Harbor, the Great Depression, World War Two and this isn't shit."

"Frank, please," Marjory said, shocked by Frank's attitude.

"Marj, you know Nic, he's a bit paranoid."

"So I'm taking that as a firm no?" Nicholas asked sarcastically.

"Wait a moment, Nic," Marjory said and turned to face

Frank. "Stop being so stubborn. You don't even know what's going on."

"We'll be fine. I'm not saying what happened wasn't bad, but it's not the end of the country."

Nicholas watched the two bicker. He imagined this was a common occurrence outside of the times he and Becky witnessed them arguing.

As they went back and forth, Nicholas looked around the quaint and always extremely clean kitchen. If Marjory was anything, she was organized. Nicholas appreciated that and was thankful that it had worn off on Becky.

"No, Marjory, we'll be fine!" Frank barked and broke Nicholas' wandering thoughts.

Marjory cringed and sheepishly replied to Frank, "Okay."

Nicholas looked at what were decades-old expressions and lines of living with a crass man. His heart tugged for her just then. For an extended second his gaze remained unblinking on her face. A deep vertical line pulled between his brows and he turned towards Frank and gave him a stare that met the man's bloodshot eyes.

"Frank…"

"What?" he asked, sitting the glass on the counter.

Nicholas could feel his blood boil, but getting angry himself wouldn't do anything to help the situation. He stopped short of expressing eighteen years of frustration, anger and spite towards the man who was his beloved's father. "Nothing, it's nothing."

A devilish grin crossed Frank's wrinkled and leathered face.

An intense urge to knock Frank's coffee-stained teeth gripped him, but the realities of doing such a thing was impossible.

"Marjory, I don't know how you can contact us, but what I'll do is stop by every day to check on you two."

Frank walked up to Nicholas and said, "You'll be just wasting your time. We'll be fine."

"Anyway, I'll try to get over here every day about this time until this clears up. Please feel free to come to our place anytime you need to. Our house is your house."

Marjory extended her shaking hand and rubbed Nicholas' arm. "You're so sweet, but like Frank said, we'll be fine."

"There's another reason I'm here," Nicholas said.

"Go ahead," Frank asked.

"Do you still have that old Dodge Dart?"

"Yeah, the old girl is out in the garage, why?"

"I think he loves that hunk of junk more than he loves me," Marjory joked.

"She doesn't give me any lip," Frank shot back.

"That rust bucket is a money hole."

"It gives me a hobby."

"Could I borrow it?" Nicholas interjected loudly over their quibbling.

Frank narrowed his eyes at Nicholas and paused for an uncomfortable amount of time before saying, "What do you need it for? You have those fancy German cars."

"It's what I've been telling you, our cars aren't working, but I think the Dart might."

"Oh, c'mon, Frank, he needs it for his family. Let him

borrow the car," Marjory said.

Frank's eyes were still slits, as he wouldn't stop leering at Nicholas.

"Frank, can I please use the car?" Nicholas asked.

"Yeah, sure, let me go get you the keys."

Frank exited the kitchen.

"You sure you don't want to come with me? Becky would love having you stay over."

Hearing this, she gripped his arm firmly. This was her way of silently telling him yes.

Her eyes gave a different answer than her voice. She loved Frank, but his inability to warm up to people damaged many relationships they'd had over the years.

Frank swept into the kitchen, holding a rabbit's-foot keychain with two keys. "Here, don't put a scratch on it and please bring it back full."

Outside, he stood holding his bike and looked back at the condo. A few more elderly people came strolling by, no apparent concern as they walked their dogs, chatting and laughing. A thought struck him; maybe he was too paranoid and this was all going to be remedied? But quickly he dashed that thought. He had become successful because of his gut instincts and street smarts. His experiences of people and the general public told him that if things didn't get fixed right away, the situation could get out of control. He understood Frank's insistence that all would be fine, but he also could see the opposite. His entire life he used this broad and open view to formulate how he should conduct himself. From business to his personal life, he always liked to cover all possible contingencies, so while he understood

Frank's position, he also found it foolish, because if Frank was wrong, it could cost him his life. If he was wrong, then he had a lot of cool gear and copious amounts of food and water.

Nicholas approached the garage door and realized that without power he wasn't getting in.

No sooner had he come to this realization than Frank hollered, "I think you'll need this to get in." He was holding up another set of keys and promptly walked towards the rear of the detached garage.

Nicholas followed.

"I mean it when I said no scratches," Frank grumbled.

"Let's just see if it runs first," Nicholas said as he stepped past Frank into the dark garage. He disengaged the automatic garage door opener and lifted the door.

Light splashed on Frank's Chevy Impala, his and Marjory's primary vehicle, and the Dodge Dart covered in a tan car cover.

Frank pulled the cover off and folded it up neatly.

Nicholas was impressed with how mint the car looked. Frank had done wonders in keeping the old car running and in good shape.

Caressing the front quarter panel, Frank purred, "I've had this beauty for a long time. I think I told you, I bought her brand new, only six miles on the odometer when I rolled off the lot with her."

"I'll take good care of it, I promise," Nicholas said. He meant what he said, but deep down he didn't know if that would come true.

The door sounded heavy when Frank opened it. He

settled in snugly behind the large steering wheel and inserted the key.

Nicholas closed his eyes and mumbled a prayer under his breath.

Frank clicked the ignition forward and pressed the accelerator slightly. The car rumbled and started.

Nicholas exhaled heavily, looked up and said, "Thank you."

"I told you she'd start up," Frank said proudly, a gleam in his eye.

"Do you have the keys for the Impala?" Nicholas asked. He was curious if it would start too.

"You know, come to think of it, why don't you take it instead?" Frank said, tossing him a set of keys.

Nicholas got behind the wheel of the 2008 Impala and put the keys in the ignition and again said a prayer. "One, two, three," he said and turned the key.

Nothing, it was dead.

"I knew it!" he said loudly.

"Impossible, I just took it out yesterday. Get out. You're doing something wrong," Frank barked.

Nicholas happily got out.

Frank got in and tried several times before yelling at the car, "Goddamn piece of junk. They don't make cars like they used to."

"Frank, this is what I've been telling you; most cars aren't working. I don't know what would cause that, but that, the power not working, and our cell phones being dead all lead to one thing."

"Hmm, there has to be a reasonable explanation."

"There is, we've been attacked by some weapon."

Frank's jaw tensed as he grinded his teeth.

"I don't know if I can let you take the Dart until I can get this started," Frank said and got out. He popped the trunk and pulled out a set of jumper cables.

"You're wasting your time, Frank. Please listen to me."

Ignoring Nicholas, Frank mumbled, "I must've left a light on. I bet Marj left the overhead on; she does that all the time. Damn fool woman."

Shaking his head in disbelief, Nicholas watched Frank unsuccessfully try to jump the Impala.

A half hour went by watching Frank curse, pound his fist and slam car doors before Nicholas spoke up. "Frank, Dad, please stop. It's not going to work. Why won't you listen to me?"

"Because you're a damn fool!"

"I can't deal with this shit one more second," Nicholas said, waving his arms in a sign of defeat. He exited the garage and grabbed his bike. He was done; he couldn't take Frank's ignorance anymore.

"Where are you going?" Frank yelled.

"I'm going home."

"I thought you wanted to use the Dodge?"

"I do, but I don't want to wait till next week to get it," Nicholas said with a snarky tone.

"Take it. Just stop by Auto Zone and pick me up a new battery for the Chevy."

Nicholas wanted to slap Frank repeatedly. He couldn't understand why he wouldn't listen. As he fumed at Frank, Nicholas took notice of a few cars with their hoods up at a set of detached garages a block away. There was no doubt that whatever happened was widespread, but just how large was the problem? Did it only encompass San Diego or was it statewide? God forbid, he thought, if it was national.

"Nic, here," Frank said. He had exited the garage and was standing next to him.

Lost in his thoughts, Nicholas turned and said, "Look over there."

Frank did and said, "Well, I'll be, looks like others are having car trouble."

Nicholas couldn't help but wonder if Frank's stubbornness wasn't senility. He snatched the keys from his hand, got in the Dodge and drove off.

San Diego, CA

Once inside, the scene was even more chaotic. One problem was that most of the store was dark save for the little light coming in from the setting sun. For an instant Bryn paused. Going into complete darkness seemed stupid at best, but if this scene was playing out everywhere else, then their opportunity to get food was possibly limited to what was in this store.

What also scared her was people's frantic reaction to the outage. She recognized that humans were pack animals and reacted to others in chorus much like a flock of birds do as they fly and turn through the air. For whatever reason, people were in a panic, and that emotion just fed on itself.

Some inside the store had flashlights. She could see the lights darting around, their beams bouncing off the aisles, ceiling and floor. She'd give anything at the moment to have a light much less something more lethal to carry for protection than her small canister of pepper spray. A strong sensation of vulnerability overcame her because she felt completely unprepared. Everything happening was surreal, and in that moment she had a nagging feeling that she was going to die.

"Are we going or what?" Sophie asked, urging them to move.

This question shattered her doubts and propelled her into the store. "Everyone stay together, okay."

"But I think we can get more if we separate," Matt chimed in.

"Fine, you go, but Sophie, you're coming with me," Bryn ordered. Seeing a cart next to one of the checkout counters, she grabbed it and with Sophie next to her went into the darkness.

Matt took off in the opposite direction. He seemed to know where he was going, but he lacked a cart. Bryn noticed this, but didn't have time to think about it. All she could do was focus on what she and Sophie needed to do.

"Do you know where we're going?" Sophie said loudly to overcome how loud it was inside. Screams, cries and hollering were coming from every direction as people battled for what they could find in the dark.

"Let's get canned food," Bryn blurted out.

As if on autopilot, she navigated the cart to the aisle

where the main bulk of canned foods were located. While her internal sense of direction was good, the trouble came from people and debris. It seemed as if every couple feet they went, someone ran into them or their cart's wheels hit something on the floor. Their eyes had adjusted to the faint light, but it was still inadequate.

"I think this is the soup aisle. Grab what you can on the shelves, hurry!" Bryn commanded.

Sophie obeyed and began to sweep up what cans she could feel on the shelves and tossed them into the cart.

Bryn followed and scooped up whatever she felt without regard for what it was. She just hoped it wasn't can after can of chicken broth. Surprising to her, there were still a good number of cans, so within ten minutes they had filled up the cart.

"Matt!" she hollered out.

"Let's get more!" Sophie barked and took off towards the entrance to find another cart.

"Sophie, no!" Bryn screamed; fear that something would happen to her filled her mind. "Sophie, come back, now!"

It was too late; she was gone.

Bryn stood, peering out, hoping she would catch a glimpse of her. She thought about following, but she didn't know exactly where she went.

"Sophie, Matt!" she called out, but no reply came. All she heard were the steady grumblings and screaming from others in the store.

"Help, Bryn, help!" echoed in the store.

With no concern for the food they had just gathered,

Bryn ran in the direction of Sophie's screaming.

"Help!"

Bryn frantically ran but couldn't find her. The last time she heard her cry it was close.

"Help!"

Bryn saw a commotion on the floor and connected that it must be her. She ran over and saw a man on top of Sophie. Not hesitating to react, Bryn jumped on the man's back and began to choke him.

"Get off of her!" Bryn barked.

The man reached back in an attempt to grab Bryn, but she wouldn't let go. Suddenly, one of his wild attempts made contact as he grasped a handful of her hair and pulled.

"Argh!" Bryn screamed out in pain.

He twisted her head and pulled her off his back. He was a large man, over two hundred and thirty pounds. He reeled back to punch her when a loud bone-crunching sound hit her ears.

Sophie had found a can of food on the floor and smashed it into the side of his head. The impact was solid, and he let out a grunt, released Bryn and slumped over.

"Oh my God, did I kill him?" Sophie asked, her voice trembling.

Bryn was furious. She snatched the can out of Sophie's hand, and if he wasn't dead, Bryn made sure he was by hitting him repeatedly while his body lay motionless on the floor.

"Bryn, Sophie, where are you?" Matt called out from inside the store.

"You alright?" Bryn asked.

"I'm fine. He tackled me is all. Nothing else happened."

"Come on," Bryn said, getting up, tossing the now bloody can and helping up Sophie.

They met up with Matt, whose scavenging had been a major success. He too had found a cart and had it full.

"Let's get the fuck out of here!" Bryn said.

"What happened?" Matt asked.

"Nothing, take Sophie outside. I'll be right back," Bryn ordered as she jogged to where she had left her cart. Fortunately it was still there, so without further delay she pushed the overburdened and heavy cart out of the store.

"Let's get home fast. Keep your eyes peeled, no bullshitting on the way home," Bryn ordered.

Sophie and Matt just nodded. The joking and petty conversations were absent on the slow walk back. The reality of the situation they had just endured penetrated deeply. None of them talked. They all pondered the new world around them and wondered if this was a temporary thing or if things had changed forever.

Carlsbad, CA

"Where's Mom and Dad?" Becky asked, cornering him the moment he walked into the house.

"I tried."

"You didn't try hard enough," she snapped.

"It's your dad, you know him," Nicholas said in his defense. He pushed past her and walked into the kitchen. A tall glass of water stared at him, so he picked it up and drank it.

She walked up behind him and rested her head between his shoulder blades. Gently she wrapped her arms around his torso and pulled him in tight.

"Honey, I tried, but he's a stubborn old man."

"I believe you. I'm just worried for them," she said.

"I know you are. I promise I'll go back tomorrow and try again."

"Well, at least we accomplished something. My pack is done and in the garage."

"Good, what about Abigail?"

"She won't stop trying to get her phone to work."

"I need your help. I'm going to push the BMW out of the garage so I can get the Dodge in. I don't need what must be one of the few cars that work to get taken."

"Who's going to take it? We live in a gated community."

He craned his head around till he could see her and said, "Trust me; you should have seen all the people gawking at me as I drove that beast home. It's a prized commodity."

"What are we going to do going forward?"

"Just sit tight."

"How do you think your brother's doing?" Becky asked, referencing Michael, Nicholas' older brother, who lived in Northern Virginia. Nicholas would joke that all they knew about him was he worked for one of the alphabet agencies.

"He's a big tough guy; I'm not worried about him."

She turned him around so they were looking at each other. "Nic, I'm scared. This whole thing is so weird. I want to think that the government will fix this, but I just don't know if that's going to happen."

"I say this not to freak you out, but we should be worried. I need to find a way to get out of here. We need to leave and soon."

"Go where?"

"I've been thinking, and your uncle has a place in the desert. We could go there."

"The desert?"

"It might be better than here; I just don't feel completely safe staying here for too long."

"I'm not sure about that. You know Uncle Jim; he's a bit touchy about anyone using his place."

"He's not there; he's up in Montana. Listen, I don't know how long we'll be safe here if the power stays off for a long time and no one comes to help."

"But if we're leaving, my parents are coming with us," Becky insisted.

"I can't guarantee that. I can't keep waiting for them, especially your father, to listen to reason. I can't let his ignorance put my family in jeopardy."

"We're not leaving without them."

"We've had this discussion before. Your parents sat in this house not nine months ago and told me they think all the stuff I was doing was crazy and that *if* it ever came to it, they'd rather die than live in a world where survival was key."

"I don't care what they said then, they're my parents."

Nicholas wanted to argue, but he knew it wouldn't solve anything. It was hard to rationalize when people were emotional, so he moved onto something else. "How's Abby? Please tell me she's not trying to take her entire wardrobe."

"She's scared; she's worried about her friends. She's just scared, period."

"Should I go talk to her?"

"I'd say yes, but don't take this the wrong way. I think your intense response to this makes her feel uneasy."

He pulled away and faced her. "What does that mean?"

"Don't take it personally, but you're an intense guy, and she knows if you're concerned, it's something to be worried about."

"You make it sound like I'm doing something wrong."

"No, please don't take it that way. I just think she needs to process whatever this is."

"I understand," he said and pulled away.

"Where are you going?"

"To my office. I need to inventory our weapons."

"Says the guy whose not intense," she joked. She snatched his shirt and pulled him back. "Don't run off without a kiss at least."

He gave in to her like he usually did and lost himself for a moment. If it wasn't for her stopping, the kiss could have easily turned to foreplay.

"Now go to work. Stop loitering around the house," she said and smacked him on the butt.

JOHN W. VANCEsegment>

With a raised eyebrow he responded, "Yes, ma'am."

Nicholas inventoried what he called his 'arsenal of freedom'. He had always loved firearms since before the Marines and had collected a really nice variety of handguns and long guns.

With a look of admiration he stood above his weapons perfectly aligned by size. On the left he had seven handguns, three Sig Sauers, one Kimber and two Smith and Wesson revolvers. On the right he had rifles and two shotguns. At the top was a Sig Sauer Model 716 .308 caliber AR platform rifle, his latest addition, below that he had an AR-15, Winchester Model 70, a Ruger 77/22 and a Remington 870 pump shotgun. For him his collection of firearms gave him some peace of mind, but no gun in the world could save you if you weren't trained in their use.

One by one he took the weapons and placed them around the house in secure locations. Having them in the safe was no longer prudent; he didn't know who might come knocking. As he walked through the darkening house, clanking came from the kitchen where Becky was attempting to make something.

She had taken up refuge there. Large southwestern-facing windows framed the space; this provided a blast of warmth and light from the descending sun.

Nicholas laughed about how the media would be reporting this situation, if they were. He imagined he'd only hear frenzy sprinkled with tidbits of useful information. A chuckle leapt from his mouth when he visualized them

80

running political interference for the administration and attempting to deflect any blame that would come while simultaneously not trying to lay blame at the feet of Islamists even if it was obvious they had done it. The big question was *who* was behind this? It made sense it was Islamic terrorists, but it could be someone else without a doubt. The relationship between Russia and the United States had deteriorated considerably over the past seven years, and the most recent drop in oil prices had crushed Russia. Or it could be China, he thought. Yes, they needed the United States to be buyers of their products but there wasn't any dispute that the ideological differences between both countries were immense. But for Nicholas, who did it was less important than what he needed to do so he and his family would survive.

"Dinner's ready!" Becky called.

Nicholas walked in and opened the freezer, took out a pint of melting vanilla ice cream and sat down at the center kitchen island.

"Don't eat that. I made dinner," Becky said.

"It's melting, don't want it to go to waste," he replied as he shoved a large spoonful of dripping ice cream into his mouth.

"I wish we had generators," Becky said.

Abigail was sitting next to her mother, but she might as well have been a thousand miles away. Her mind could only think about her friends but more specifically, Rob Robles. Rob was a year older than her and unbeknownst to her parents, he was her boyfriend.

Frustrated, she let out a grunt then tossed her phone

on the counter.

"You can keep trying, but your phone is dead, caput, fried, burned out," Nicholas commented.

"I hate hearing myself talk. Are you listening to me?" Becky scolded Nicholas.

"Generators, I know, I heard you."

"Why didn't you buy some of those?"

"This coming from the woman who rolled her eyes every time I went to a gun show or prepper show to get gear. Now you question why I didn't do something. Honey, you need to be happy I got what I got. The food will last us a while."

"Then what?" she asked.

He looked at her and wanted to give her an answer that would give her and him comfort, but she was right, then what? "I'll make a run to a store tomorrow and see if I can scrounge up anything," he said and went back to the freezer and opened it up. He took out two more pints of ice cream and gave one to Becky and one to Abigail.

Abigail looked at it and smiled.

Becky asked, "What are you doing?"

"Eat the ice cream. Enjoy it. Come on, sit down, pop open the top and enjoy what might be the last ice cream you have in a long time. Let's make tonight just about us. Let's talk and have fun."

Becky looked at him and her concern began to wane.

"I think I've done all I can do for now. Let's take the time to be with each other. I don't know what's going to happen tomorrow or after, but right now I have the two most important people in my life right here."

His sentimental comments struck a chord in Abigail. She walked over and put her arms around him. Resting her head against his broad shoulders, she said, "I love you, Daddy."

Nicholas raised his left arm and beckoned for Becky to come.

She did.

They embraced firmly and exchanged kisses and laughs. Nicholas appreciated this moment because he feared that it might soon be one of their last peaceful moments together.

USS *Harpers Ferry*, Sixty Miles off the Coast of Southern California

The mess hall reverberated with the sounds of hundreds of Marines and sailors discussing the topic that was undeniably the issue of their lifetimes.

Vincent looked around for a place to sit, but seats were a rare commodity.

"Sergeant Vincent, over here!" Berg, his driver, hollered from across the space.

Vincent's military occupational specialty was a heavy machine gunner. He manned a Browning M2 .50 caliber machine gun and was the squad leader for his combined arms team. While deployed with the MEU (Marine Expeditionary Unit) many Marines were given secondary missions and responsibilities. His was the team leader for a

TRAP team; these are small squad-sized elements whose responsibility was to recover downed pilots. He enjoyed this special-operations-capable mission above his job as a machine gunner. Vincent rose to leadership positions because of his dedication to all things Corps, but now he couldn't wait to leave. He had fallen asleep thinking about his parents and woke with those same thoughts plaguing him. What his new mission would entail was vexing, and with the country hurtling towards chaos, he didn't know when he'd ever make it back.

"Over here," Berg again called out, waving his arm.

Vincent strolled over, tossed his tray on the table and took a seat.

"Not hungry?" Berg asked after seeing Vincent's tray was practically empty.

"I'm tired of this slop."

"God, I know, I was so looking forward to an In-N-Out burger, oh, and a carne asada burrito from Alberto's."

"That does sound good."

"What do you think is going to happen?" Berg asked.

"I don't know, but it can't be good. According to you, this thing was big. All I know is most people act like fucking animals when they can't get Wi-Fi or they miss breakfast at McDonald's. Take away power…"

"Turn off their phones, Christ, they'll eat each other alive," Berg cracked, stuffing a forkful of pasta in his mouth.

"So true, take their phones away, they'll have a riot."

"I wonder how my girlfriend is doing. I bet she's freaking out."

"I hope she's good. You worried?"

"Yeah, but she has family and they're in a small town. I kinda think small towns can manage things like this better."

Vincent thought about Berg's comment. It was probably true. His parents too lived in a small town. Their ability to work with local authorities and know everyone would be beneficial say over a large city like San Diego with over two million people, most of whom didn't keep more than a week's worth of food on hand. This gave him a bit of peace knowing his parents were able people and the town manageable.

"What I'm worried about is she'll hang herself over the fact she won't be able to watch her reality shows." Berg laughed.

"Now she's starring in her own reality show called the apocalypse."

"Oh shit, man, this really throws a wrench in my plans this weekend, but this can be fun."

"In what way?" Vincent asked.

"We're one step closer to a zombie apocalypse. People will go fucking crazy, start ripping and tearing at each other, and we can sit back and kick these civilians' asses once and for all."

"I've never heard you spout such contempt before," Vincent commented.

"C'mon, Sergeant Vincent, don't you tire of the self-righteous attitudes of civvies? We protect their rights to say stupid shit about us. But if we want to have a say in something or offer an opinion or say something political, we're told we can't. Ha, we can't? We're the motherfuckers who protect that right, but we can't participate, such bullshit!"

Vincent watched Berg's nostrils flare and eyes widen as he waved his arms around.

"Look, that's the system and we volunteered. If you don't like it, then don't re-enlist, then you can be that asshole out there talking trash."

"That was my plan, but do you think they're going to be letting any of us out? Nope, today marks six months and a wake-up and my enlistment is up, but I think I'm here to stay for the duration of whatever is happening out there."

"Don't be so negative. Christ, Berg, by then they'll figure this stuff out."

Suddenly the mess hall's volume rose dramatically.

Vincent and Berg turned towards the epicenter of the raucousness. There they saw a Marine jump on top of a table. They couldn't hear what he was saying because of the jeers and yelling.

Vincent rose and walked closer.

Calls for people to be quiet grew until they were heeded. The mess fell silent.

"Everyone, listen, I just came from the ops center. Washington, DC, has been nuked, so has New York, Los Angeles, Chicago and Houston. We're at war, motherfuckers, we're at war!"

"Who, who did it?" a voice cried out.

"The Russians, but only after we nuked them."

A chorus of loud chatter erupted as Marines and sailors discussed and debated the news.

Vincent was in complete shock. First the EMP, now

five major U.S. cities had been destroyed.

Right on cue the loudspeakers came to life and a siren blared. "General quarters, general quarters."

This was it, war, but not just any war, nuclear war. Never in his life did he imagine this sort of thing could have occurred, but it had. Now without a doubt any recovery effort they'd be participating in would be futile.

Berg grabbed his arm and turned him around. "Can you believe this shit?"

Vincent's face showed his shock. His thousand-yard stare told Berg what no words could.

"You okay, Sergeant?"

"Yeah, I'm fine. I just can't fathom this."

"We gotta go, c'mon," Berg said.

Marines and sailors hurried towards their areas of responsibility. For Vincent and Berg that was to be holed up in their berthing.

As Vincent navigated the bustling passageways, he ran directly into Gunny Roberts.

"Sergeant Vincent, you're the man I needed to see. Come with me," Gunny ordered.

"Where are we going?"

"It's not where we're going, it's where are you going."

"What?"

"Son, you got a mission. You leave soon."

"Where?"

"You and your TRAP team are headed to San Marcos."

"San Marcos, like east of Pendleton?"

"Yes."

"For what?"

"You're in charge of grabbing the CO's wife and kids."

San Diego, CA

The orange glow from the two dozen tealight and various other candles bounced a multitude of shadows off the walls and ceiling of Bryn's apartment. After their successful grocery-store run, she felt a sense of relief and accomplishment, enough to let her proverbial hair down to relax and drink a few hastily put together cocktails from the random assortment of liquors and mixers she had around the apartment.

With a mind towards the future, she forced Sophie to eat from among the foods that would spoil first. In her refrigerator she ate a half-eaten quesadilla while Sophie devoured the remaining rice and beans they had taken home the other night.

The cocktails gave her a reprieve from the day's stress as she laughed at Matt's silly jokes. After what they had been through at the store, she invited him over; there they would divide the spoils and just talk. Never in her life would she imagine feeling safe with him, but having him there did make her feel a bit more secure. She didn't know him well, but she felt she could trust him. Somehow he didn't give off the creep vibe like the three, Alberto, Dylan and Craig did. She trusted her intuition, as it had always served her in life, and in unsure times she planned on leaning on that sense more than ever.

"I can't say it enough, you were a total badass today," Sophie said, the few drinks already showing in her slurred speech. The fear and trauma she had experienced in the store was leaving her with each sip of her drink.

"You're like a superhero; all you need is a mask and cape!" Matt said excitedly.

"Matt, you read way too many comics," Bryn quipped and continued. "I just hate punks. Anyone that picks on the weak need to get their heads smashed in."

"Do you have training or something?" Matt asked genuinely curious.

"Nope, I just see red when those sorts of things happen and I act out without thinking."

"She's always been fiery, Matt, so get used to it," Sophie added.

"I wish I had seen you bash that guy's head in!" Matt exclaimed.

"Can we talk about something else?" Bryn asked. She didn't like to relive things with others because she would do it enough on her own.

"So where are the police?" Sophie asked.

"They're in the same situation we are," Matt answered.

"So no one is coming to help? What about the government?" Sophie asked.

"No one is coming is what I understand. I ran into a guy at the store who was going on about how terrorists attacked the country," Matt said.

"This is an attack?"

"Makes sense to me," Bryn said.

"If it's an EMP, then it only makes sense that a terrorist did it," Matt said.

"I don't understand how this could happen, none of this, how can this happen?"

"Is that a serious question?" Bryn pointedly asked.

"Don't be like that. How can this happen?" Sophie pressed.

"The fuck nuts in DC can't wipe their own asses. You honestly think they even give a shit much less planned for something like this?" Bryn challenged.

"I have to agree with Bryn on this," Matt said.

"Matt, so you think the power's not coming back on…at all?" Sophie asked.

"I don't know what really happened, but this looks like an EMP to me."

"What are we going to do?" Sophie asked.

"Getting more food is important," Bryn answered.

"We should go to Mom's house," Sophie said.

"We're not going to Mom's."

"Why not? I bet she has food."

"You think she has food? You're crazy for even thinking that. You were just over there last week. She had less in her fridge than we had."

"Where does your Mom live?"

"La Jolla," Sophie said.

"You're a native San Diegan? Wow, it's like seeing a chupacabra, I didn't know you guys existed," Matt joked.

Sophie chuckled and said, "You're funny for a dork."

"Ha, is that a compliment?"

"Yeah."

"But you just called me a dork," Matt said, somewhat amused and astonished.

"Seriously, you don't know you're a dork?" Bryn quipped.

"Is that my cue to go?"

"No, don't go, I'm sorry," Sophie said.

"No wait, hold on. Matt, you don't think wearing R2-D2 and Darth Vader shirts make you a dork?" Bryn continued.

"*Star Wars* is cool!" Matt said defensively.

"It might have been a fun movie and cool when you're ten years old, but you're a grown man wearing superhero and *Star Wars* T-shirts!" Bryn blasted.

"I guess I'm a dork, then."

"I think dorks are cute," Sophie added, again slurring her speech.

"So what was your childhood like?" Matt asked Bryn directly.

Bryn, not wanting to answer the question, stood up and walked into the kitchen, leaving Sophie to give her two cents. Her mouth was a bit parched, so she turned on the spigot. Nothing came out but a strange hollow echo, like the pipes were moaning. "Shit," she bellowed and put down her cup. She opened the refrigerator to see if there was anything close to water. Nothing.

Walking back into the living room, she asked, "Did anyone grab water?"

Matt and Sophie looked at each other and shook their heads.

"Not smart. We'll need to go back out tomorrow,"

Bryn lamented.

"Just drink from the sink, little princess," Sophie joked.

"I tried. There's nothing coming out."

"Oh, that's not good. There's always the toilet," Sophie said and began to laugh loudly.

Matt followed suit with a boisterous laugh and added, "Yeah, get on all fours like my old dog and start lapping away."

"Idiots, the both of you," Bryn snapped. She unlocked the door to go outside, as she remembered she had a half a bottle of water in her car.

Matt and Sophie kept joking, but she wasn't listening anymore. She closed the door and slowly proceeded towards her car in the darkness. She paused just at the top of the stairs to allow her eyes to properly adjust. It was so strange not to have any artificial light to guide her. Comfortable to make it, she put her foot out, but a voice from the darkness stopped her.

"Watch that first step."

"Who's there?" Bryn asked, looking to her left, but only seeing the black of night.

"Your guardian angel," the male voice joked.

"No, really, who is that?" she again asked.

"Colin Somerville, your neighbor from apartment 213."

"Never heard of you. Wait, are you the old man who lives…"

"Old man? Ouch! I'm only fifty-six," Colin said.

Bryn still couldn't see him and wondered how he saw her.

With a few clicks of his lighter, the glow from the flame showed Bryn the man behind the voice. It was the 'old man' she was referring to. They knew of each other, but that was as far as their knowledge of each other went.

Colin was a retired Master Chief in the Navy. He was a big man physically, standing over six feet three inches, and had big muscular arms that hung from his massive torso like two branches from the trunk of an old tree. His bald head was covered with a perfectly folded bill ball cap that read, Vietnam Veteran. He was from a small bayou town in Louisiana and had joined the Navy instead of going to jail. The judge at the time gave him two options, go to jail for a breaking and entering charge or join the military; he opted for the military route. That was 1972, and within nine months of that decision he was in the jungles of Vietnam working as a Corpsman. The regimented lifestyle of the Navy agreed with him, so he stayed for twenty-eight years. Leaving his home and mother was tough, but she wouldn't have it any other way. She saw the Navy as a second chance for him. All she saw for his life if he stayed was jail. He had gotten in with the wrong crowd at a young age, and as a black male in the South, she just knew he needed to get out.

Colin inhaled deeply as the flame rose and fell with each breath in; when it was perfectly lit, he pulled it away and blew the smoke on the cherry tip. "I didn't catch your name."

"I'm Bryn from 207."

"Nice to meet you, Bryn. Funny it takes the lights going out for us to finally meet. Guess we can't hide in our homes anymore," Colin commented.

"Yeah, um, I need to go get something. Have a good one," Bryn said and slowly walked down the stairs.

"You too, have a good one."

Bryn carefully walked down the stairs, all the while thinking about her brief encounter. What Colin said was true. She had seen him before but not until then had she ever shared a word except to say hello. She then openly wondered what new people she'd meet now that her life had definitely taken a turn.

Darkness fell upon the city. It blanketed the towers of downtown and the hills to the east. The sky twinkled with thousands of stars and the Milky Way sliced through the center. This was a sky many had never seen before in San Diego. The hazy luminance from the city was no longer there to block out the natural beauty. And while many took time and enjoyed the uniqueness of the event, others began to plot and scheme how they could exploit the situation for their own gain.

CHAPTER TWO

"When we are no longer able to change a situation – we are challenged to change ourselves." – Viktor E. Frankl

Two Thousand Feet Above Southern California

The planning and preparation for the mission to get Captain Dupree's family took longer than they had initially planned. What had started as Dupree's personal mission had morphed into an MEU-wide rescue for all the officers' and senior non-commissioned officers' families. In order to facilitate such a large-scale operation, they needed great coordination. Not an impossible task; it just required more time.

Vincent's mission hadn't changed. He and his team were to grab Mrs. Dupree and their two young children, a boy and girl, aged six and eight.

The CH-53E Super Stallion with Vincent and his team lifted off the rear flight deck at zero five thirty.

One man absent from the team was Lance Corporal Berg. As the team was headed to the assembly area, he slipped and fell down the ladder well, injuring his leg and making his ability to go impossible. For Vincent this was a loss, but overcoming and adapting was something the Marines did.

95

Vincent looked at his men, a somber but determined look on their faces. Going into situations like this wasn't new for them. They had just completed several months of combat in Afghanistan in support of another Marine Infantry Battalion.

This mission should be easy, they told him, but the second he heard that, he knew it could be their curse.

The cool fresh air mixed with the helicopter's fumes, a smell he had become accustomed to. The heavy rhythmic thumping from the rotor often lulled some Marines to sleep. For him this never occurred; his mind was always processing and visualizing the mission at hand. He would run through every scenario possible and play out exactly how he needed it to go down. Sleep was something for those who didn't have responsibility.

Vincent looked over his shoulder and noticed they had banked and now were heading south.

"Sergeant Vincent, this is First Lieutenant Prince. We're ten mikes out," the pilot said in Vincent's headset.

"Roger that," Vincent replied. He lifted up his hands showing ten fingers and motioned to his Marines. This was their sign they were ten minutes away.

Behind Vincent was a small window; he turned to look out. As they flew past familiar landmarks, Vincent reminisced briefly about the world before. One thing that was obvious was the lack of artificial light. The city and suburbs were dark, and as they flew over Interstate 5, he saw thousands of stalled and abandoned cars.

Prince lowered the helicopter, signaling their final approach.

Their altitude was low enough for Vincent to see a small group of people, a dozen at least, gathered along a small surface street. He saw they were pointing at them and making hand and arm gestures. Vincent looked more intently and saw they had rifles. Really focusing on them, he noticed two of them had the rifles on their shoulders. Streaks of flashes erupted from the muzzles, confirming these men were shooting at them.

The helicopter banked hard away from the group and headed east.

Loud panging on the lower fuselage rang out. Marines looked around at each other, nervous that they were under fire.

The helicopter suddenly went higher; Prince was attempting to pull away.

A minute went by with no panging or diversionary maneuvers. Vincent let out a heavy breath and said, "Damn, that was nerve-racking."

"That was nothing," Prince replied.

Vincent had forgotten he was wearing the headset and that everything he said the pilot, co-pilot and crew chief heard.

"I'm sure, but being a passenger can make you a bit more anxious."

"We're fine. We'll have you on the ground in five mikes," Prince said.

The helicopter banked back south and again began its descent when without notice it shuddered and dropped, causing a feeling of weightlessness.

To Vincent it felt like the helicopter had lost power as

they kept falling.

With a grinding jolt, the propeller turbine came to life again, stopping their fall but only for a moment before he heard the engine cease again.

Several Marines cried out in fear they were going down.

The jolting had pushed a couple Marines off the webbing and onto the floor.

One was Private First Class Temple, a young nineteen-year-old Marine from Biloxi, Mississippi. Vincent liked him a lot; it was probably because he could see himself in Temple.

Vincent unbuckled and went to his aid. "Here, grab my arm."

Black smoke entered the helicopter from outside.

Seeing this distressed the men more.

Vincent found it almost impossible to balance himself as the helicopter continued its uncontrolled fall. The decision to help Temple, while brave, was not a wise decision, Vincent suddenly thought.

The helicopter jerked hard and began to spin, throwing Vincent to the floor hard. He rolled across the floor and slammed into the webbing. He reached out and grabbed it to hold himself.

The helicopter was now on its side. He looked up and could see the ground closing fast through the open window

More shuddering and the engine fired up again. The helicopter stabilized but was not far off the ground. He crawled up onto the webbing and looked out the window. They couldn't be more than two hundred feet from the ground. A fear gripped him like none he'd ever experienced. He thought that after all the combat and being so close to home that this was how he would die, and to add insult to injury it was at the hands of Americans.

Two minutes passed and it seemed like the worst was over. The helicopter was stable and they were flying although low to the ground, but smoke was still billowing into the fuselage.

Vincent thought it safe to get back in his seat when suddenly an explosion rocked the rear of the helicopter. It blew off the rear section, including the lift ramp, vaporizing the crew chief in the fiery blast.

The explosion caused catastrophic damage to the tail section by shearing off the rear stabilizing prop. There was nothing that could save the helicopter as gravity took over.

Violently it began to spin.

Vincent desperately tried to hold on to the webbing, but the force of the spin threw him towards the rear and out of the helicopter.

As he tumbled through the emptiness, he saw the intense blue of the sky, then the tans, browns and greens of the ground. A strange thought came to mind as he fell, *'Is this going to hurt?'* With intense anticipation he closed his eyes and prayed.

San Diego, CA

Bryn tried to block out Matt's loud snoring, but with every

labored breath he took, it sounded like a freight train was barreling down on her. In frustration she got out of her bed and walked into the living room. There on the floor, Matt was sprawled out, his head propped up by a small pillow from the couch and his jacket as a blanket. Sophie was on the couch, passed out and apparently deaf to Matt's trumpeting nose. Not able to deal with his snoring and seeing the bright sun of the late morning coming through the blinds, she walked over and kicked him.

"Get up or turn over, but stop fucking snoring," Bryn said.

Matt shot up, his eyes wide open. He sniffled and wiped his face quickly then focused on Bryn, "What is it? Is everything okay?"

"No, it's not okay; your snoring is too loud."

Bryn walked into the kitchen, where she found the bottle of water from her car. She drank the rest and put it down. Today, they'd have to go find water and more food if they could. "Get up. Come on, we need to go get some water," she said and tossed the empty plastic bottle at Sophie. It hit her, but she didn't move.

"She's out. I've never seen girls drink like you two," Matt commented, standing up and stretching.

"Where should we go?" Bryn asked, ignoring his comment.

"Best Buy," Matt answered.

"Best Buy?"

"Yeah, they have food, snack food, but there's water, cases of it."

Bryn hadn't thought about that, but she did remember

that they had coolers and a full aisle of junk food near the checkout counters.

"I even have a way in," he said, holding up a large key.

It took them over an hour to finally leave the apartment, and when they did, they found their neighbors still doing pretty much what they had done the day before. Many were sitting around talking about the rumors of a massive terrorist attack and the possibility that the lights would be out for some time. They heard that a few of their neighbors had left to go to other relatives nearby, and others had gone out looking for help and supplies. The main thing that Bryn noticed was there was no coordinated effort. Like people had become in the modern world, many were fragmented and looked out only for themselves, not unlike what she was doing. It wasn't a natural reaction to only look out for oneself, she hadn't created a bond with anyone, and her childhood told her that she couldn't trust anyone. Just having Matt close was unlike her.

Leaning on the railing overlooking the parking lot was Colin, this time no cigar but a bottle of water. He smiled and nodded at them as they passed.

As usual, 'the three amigos', as Bryn called them, were smoking and talking at the bottom of the stairwell. They made immature comments and again tried to flirt with Sophie, who today didn't respond.

"I need to go get something," Matt said and jogged away towards his apartment.

Bryn and Sophie found the shopping carts where they

had left them last night. With nothing working, this was their only means of transporting anything.

Pulling the pepper spray from her pocket, Bryn shook it. "Damn."

"What is it?"

"Not much left, I need to find something else."

"Maybe we should carry a bat or a stick, something like that," Sophie commented.

"We need a gun," Bryn stated.

"A gun?" Sophie asked, shocked to hear Bryn mention it.

"Yes, I wish I had a gun."

"I don't think that's a good idea," Sophie said.

"You're right. It's not a good idea, it's a great idea. I wonder where I can get one." She then turned and looked up at Colin.

He was still there, leaning against the railing, and nodded.

To Bryn he seemed so calm, like none of this bothered him. She wondered to herself how he could be so at ease.

Matt ran up, huffing and puffing. "Okay, let's go."

"What did you get?" Bryn asked, curious.

"This," he responded, holding up what looked like a short black metal pipe.

"What is that?" Sophie asked.

"An ASP," he answered, then with a quick downward motion, the baton expanded in length. He held it up, waving it back and forth like a light saber, proud of his weapon.

"Nice, that will come in handy. I like you more and

more, Mateo," Bryn said with a grin on her face.

Carlsbad, CA

Nicholas didn't wait for the sun to rise; he was up and working in the garage organizing his gear when the creaking of the garage door pulled his focus towards it.

Wanting to keep what he was doing private, he didn't open the garage door, but in order to see what he was doing, he donned an LED headlamp he had stored in a large 40mm ammunition can he'd purchased at a gun show, and he had two LED lanterns on that had also been stored in the same ammunition can.

He turned the warm light on the garage house door to find Abigail standing there.

"What ya doing, Dad?" she asked.

"Just organizing things. We're going to be leaving soon, and I want to make sure we take what is critical. That old Dodge can't hold too much, so we have to be very practical."

"Oh."

"Do you want to help?" he asked.

"Can I? I don't know if I'll be any help."

"Nonsense, come in here."

She tucked her long dark hair behind her ears and stepped into the garage.

He gave her a task and she went right to doing it. As they both worked, he could feel a hesitation coming from her. It wasn't that he was clairvoyant; he was just a father who had paid close attention to his daughter all his life.

Stopping what he was doing, he looked at her. "Honey, what's wrong?"

"I'm just scared," she answered, turning to face him.

"I can understand that. What else is it?"

She looked down while chewing on her lip.

He stepped close to her and asked again, "You can tell me. You know you can trust me. I've always been there for you."

"I'm just worried for my friends."

"I'm sure they're fine."

Lifting her head, she looked at him with one eyebrow raised. "Really? No, don't you think my friends parents are, what's the word you used, dopey?"

"Are you asking me to do something, or are you just venting?"

"Now that we have a car, do you mind if we checked on them?"

He was about to say no when he hesitated. The last thing he needed was to have her worked up or angry at a time when he needed her support. Stepping back from this as a parent, he tackled it as a business professional. "Yes, but not today, I'm sure they're fine right now. I promise that before we leave—"

"When are we leaving for Uncle Jim's?"

"In a couple days, three at the most."

"Three days, why can't we stop by some of their houses when you go and check on Nana and Papa?"

"I'll see what I can do," he answered and touched her

hand.

"Thanks, Daddy," she said, a broad smile showing her delight.

"Is that it?" he asked recognizing she only used *daddy* when she wanted something.

"Um, no."

"What else?"

"You said you'll give me a gun to keep. I was wondering when I can get it."

"Yes, that. How about I talk to your mom and then I'll get you set up later this morning?"

"Perfect," she said and twirled around to go back to her inventory.

He watched her shake and dance to a tune she hummed. Pride filled him as he looked at the little girl who had been his pride and joy become the young woman who displayed the perfect blend of femininity and confident strength that she'd not seen in many men. He just needed to make sure she'd survive what might be coming, and in order to do that she had to be equipped with a new set of skills and tools.

San Diego, CA

Fortunately for them, the Best Buy where Matt worked was several miles away. The walk was uneventful, but visually entertaining. As compared to yesterday, they saw more people moving around and even spotted a few operational vehicles. They took notice that the cars were older models. Matt attributed this to the earlier models not having computers and electrical systems to operate the cars. A group of teenagers they encountered were going from abandoned car to abandoned car, breaking in and stealing what they thought was valuable. Like them, the shopping cart was the mode of transport for many out scavenging.

Matt had assumed that the store would be intact, but when they made the turn and saw the storefront, this assumption was destroyed like the front doors had been.

When they got closer, a few people were rushing out with equipment in a cart.

"Human beings are a pathetic joke. Do these people realize they're stealing junk? None of that shit will work." Bryn laughed.

"You're right. People suck," Matt said and thrust the baton till it expanded fully.

Bryn readied her pepper spray as they closed in on the front.

More people dashed out, their arms cradling Blu-ray players and game systems.

They jumped each time someone popped out of the store until they walked up and were able to get a perspective of what was going on inside.

Glass from the large sliding door was glimmering in the early afternoon sun, and each foot they planted crunched the shards into the concrete.

"There, grab that cart," Matt said, pointing at a small blue cart just inside the store. With a take-charge attitude, he then ordered, "Grab what food you can and I'll go to the back of the store for the cases of water." He quickly disappeared into the store.

Bryn and Sophie didn't debate his command and went to work on junk food. To their surprise and delight, most of it was still there. Those who had broken into the store were more interested in getting useless electrical equipment. Quickly they filled their two carts; they even began to fill their pockets with candy bars. Near the counter Bryn saw small packaged flashlights and batteries. She grabbed them all and stuffed them into the burgeoning cart.

"We'll need batteries. Grab as many as you can," Bryn ordered and dashed over to an aisle. After a moment she saw that Sophie wasn't there. She turned, fearing something had happened to her, but found her reading a magazine. "What the fuck!"

Sophie had lost herself in a magazine she had seen near the cash register. "Sorry."

"Get over here!"

A loud crash and bang came from the back of the store.

They both looked up, only to discover Matt coming their way, cart full of cases of water.

He ran up, a smile stretched across his pudgy face, and said, "Let's get this stuff back, drop off and come back. There's a shit load of stuff back there."

Seeing they were limited in their capacity, Bryn agreed, and they all went back. A second day and a second successful haul for them, but she knew this wouldn't last. She didn't want to take away from the joy of having been triumphant again, but soon and probably within days, the ease they were having would subside and then a real fight for survival would ensue.

Upon their return to Sycamore Grove, they found everything the same as they had left it. People still stood around, some were working on their cars, the cries of hungry babies could be heard from a few open windows, kids were playing outside and the three amigos were still sitting at the bottom of the stairs smoking.

"Whoa, look at you guys," Alberto said out loud, excited to see the carts full of food and water. "I'm hungry. Can I have a package of the Bugles?"

"No," Bryn quickly snapped.

"What?" he asked surprised.

"If you're hungry, go get your own food."

"C'mon, Bryn, don't be that way," Sophie said as she reached and took a bag of Bugles and gave it to him.

"How about me?" Dylan then said.

"Absolutely not. Sophie, no more, this is ours, we got it. If you want food, go get some," Bryn barked as she stepped from behind her cart and snatched the bag of chips Sophie was offering Dylan.

"Why you bein' a bitch, yo?" Alberto bellowed.

"I'm not. I just don't believe in rewarding laziness."

"You callin' me lazy?"

"I think you can figure that out yourself. Your ass hasn't left these stairs since the power went out yesterday morning," Bryn shot back.

"Fuck you, bitch!" Alberto fired back, now standing

and thrusting his arms around in a wild display.

"Get out of our way. We need to unload our stuff," Bryn ordered.

Matt just watched the verbal back and forth and didn't get involved. Alberto and his friends intimidated him, and he felt they would kick his ass.

"I'm not getting outta the way. You want to go up, pay a toll," Alberto said. He was still standing and put his arms out so that she couldn't get by.

"Get out of the way, Alberto," Bryn said, clearly irritated by him.

Sophie too kept quiet. She knew her sister, and there was no having her back down from an altercation.

Bryn grabbed a case of water and walked up to within inches of Alberto and stopped when he wouldn't move. "Get out of the way."

"No."

"Alberto, move."

Dylan and Craig now stood in solidarity with their friend and smiled devilishly at Bryn.

"Get out of my way," Bryn said as she now pushed against Alberto to move.

Alberto didn't budge. He laughed, and then shoved Bryn. She stumbled back a few feet and ran into the cart.

She looked down and began to shake her head. That feeling, that overwhelming feeling of rage began to fill her, starting in her head and moving down. She placed the case of water back in the cart and then reached for the pepper spray in her pocket when a metal snapping sound got her attention. She looked over and saw Matt standing tall with his baton fully extended in his hand.

"Leave her alone," he barked.

Alberto laughed, then said, "Look at Pillsbury Dough Boy acting all tough."

Craig stepped out from behind Alberto, pulled out a knife and said, "C'mon, tubby."

"Guys, stop, everybody stop!" Sophie screamed.

"Shut up, little sweet cheeks!" Alberto mockingly spouted.

"That's it," Bryn said, pulling the pepper spray out, but stopped when she heard a shotgun's action work.

Looking up, she saw Colin at the top of the steps, his shotgun pointed at the backs of the three amigos. "If you boys want to see tomorrow much less the next few minutes, you'll close your mouths, put your knives away and do as the young lady asked. Get out of their way."

Dylan turned and saw Colin holding the shotgun. He hollered, "The old man has a gun. Berto, the old man has a gun!"

Alberto and Craig turned to see the same view, the muzzle of a 12-gauge Remington 870 pointed at them.

"Put the gun down, poppy!" Alberto said.

"You boys need to find another place to loiter. Now move."

Alberto just stared at Colin, their eyes locked in a bitter contest to see who'd budge first.

"Don't tempt me. I'm an old vet who has PTSD; I'll put you down like a pack of wild dogs. Now get moving," Colin said, his steely eyes not moving from his first target, Alberto.

Bryn, Matt and Sophie just stood voyeuristically watching the standoff.

Alberto knew he couldn't win, especially if Colin was determined to use the shotgun. Conceding, he turned to his two friends and said, "Let's go, fuck these motherfuckers."

The three looked at each other and strutted off. Just before Alberto cleared the corner of their building, he turned and flipped his middle finger at Bryn and Colin.

Bryn picked up the case of water and marched up the stairs; she stopped at the top and looked at Colin, who was now relaxing in a chair. She said, "Thank you."

"My pleasure, I always hated those punks; glad they're not over here stinking up the place."

Bryn smiled and walked to her front door. She unlocked it and was about to walk in when Colin stopped her by saying, "You watch yourself, okay? This wasn't the last time you'll have to deal with them."

Bryn looked at him and answered, "Yeah, I figured. So how can a girl like me get her hands on a gun like that?"

"Oh, that?" He motioned with a slight grin. "You don't want that, but I might have something else that's better suited for ya. Come by later, I'll get you outfitted."

"Sounds like a plan."

San Felipe, Mexico

The small bedroom was exactly fifteen paces wide, and by the late morning Michael had walked that span forty times.

Not wasting any time, he got up the moment the sun's rays came through the blinds. Overnight, more of his memory had returned, but when asked by Marco, he denied knowing anything.

His memory of being a Ranger had come back to him completely as did a lot of his past. He remembered that his brother, Nicholas, lived just north of San Diego and that he was his only family. While he paced the tiny space, he calculated his escape. He'd wait for the right moment and slip past Marco, preferably while his captor was asleep.

The door handle turned.

Not wanting to appear too healthy, he jumped back in bed and lay there.

The door opened fully. It was Marco and he was holding a tray of food.

"Here," he said, placing the tray next to his bed. "You remember anything else?"

"Nothing really, I do remember washing up on shore, but nothing about a ship or missile."

"Keep trying," Marco said and left, slamming the door behind him.

Michael had to get out of this situation and fast.

The rumble of a truck engine got his attention; he got out of bed and peeked through the blinds. There in the driveway he saw Jose, Maria, a woman who must have been Jose's wife, and a small Datsun truck. They got in and drove off. As a trail of dust followed behind them, Michael prayed they were coming back because that little white truck was his way out of here.

Somberness came over him. He couldn't figure out

what he was doing on that ship and exactly what had happened. From the little he was told, a missile had been fired and now the grid was down in San Felipe. He knew what the missile represented and what had created the blackout. During his years in the Army, EMPs were discussed during the nuclear, biological and chemical courses he had taken. He recalled that the use of an EMP typically preceded a major nuclear strike. Is that what had happened? Had a nuclear war broken out? But why was he in Mexico, and why would he have been on the ship?

He laughed out loud when he thought that he had as many questions that needed answering as Manuel, Marco or the others had.

He looked around the sparse room for something he could use as a weapon. If he was going to make a daring escape, he'd need something to fight with. In the room there was a full-size bed with no headboard or footboard, a nightstand with only a Bible in the single drawer, a small lamp and a four-drawer dresser. Pulling out the drawers from the dresser was disappointing, as he only found clothes. "If I were a makeshift weapon, where would I be?" he asked himself. He scanned the room again, and when his eyes came upon the closet, they opened wide. It took him two steps to get there, he flung open the door, but the closet held nothing but boxes of blankets. Frustrated, he closed the door and rested his head against the wall. He turned, saw the crucifix and said a prayer, and as if God answered him, his eyes looked squarely at the framed Jesus that hung opposite the crucifix. He took it off the wall, removed the back and popped out the glass. He reassembled it and got it back on the wall. He placed the five-by-eight-inch glass under a pillow and broke it. Using the linen napkin that came with his meal, he wrapped it around the base and created a handle.

Holding his improvised dagger, he felt empowered and one step closer to freedom.

Thoughts of his brother then flooded in. He now recalled that Nicholas had a family and that he had a niece. A sense of obligation and protection hit him. Escape took on greater meaning. He needed to help his brother, and he needed to be in San Diego protecting them against whatever had been unleashed. He just prayed that he wasn't behind the hell that had been let loose.

Carlsbad, CA

"Absolutely not!" Becky declared.

"Becky, please, it makes sense," Nicholas replied defensively, his temples throbbing from the stressful and dramatic debate.

"Mom, don't be like this," Abigail pleaded.

"No, no, no. My little girl is not going to be running around with a gun."

"I need her to be able to defend herself," Nicholas fired back.

"From what, huh? The world isn't falling apart like you thought it would. Maybe, just maybe things will get back to normal soon."

"You're being ridiculous, you really are," Nicholas barked.

"Mom, c'mon, what if something happens or I'm by myself?"

"That's not going to happen and, honey, what if you do something stupid with it?"

"I'll train her, make sure she knows what she's doing with it," Nicholas said in an attempt to find a compromise.

"Dad took me to the range a few times. I know how to shoot," Abigail said.

"That's in a controlled environment, Abby, not walking around with a loaded gun," Becky fired back.

"Becky, I'm giving her a revolver. It's simple to use and she won't have any issues and that's that," Nicholas declared, putting his foot down and establishing that he was in control.

Becky's eyes grew to look like two saucers. The veins in her neck bulged and her nostrils flared. Her anger was near a tipping point. "If you give her a gun…"

Nicholas leaned in; he wanted to hear what her ultimatum would be.

Her eyes shifted as she searched her mind for a proper punishment.

"Abby, come with me," Nicholas ordered and headed for his office, Abigail in tow.

"Don't you dare!" Becky yelled.

"Or what? I won't be around to always protect you guys. This is important."

Becky looked at them as they walked towards Nicholas' office. If she had a gun herself, she'd probably shoot

Nicholas.

"Nic, we had an agreement," she stated.

"Not when it comes to protecting my family," he said, not stopping.

Becky huffed and followed them into his office.

The safe door was open and he was pulling out two small plastic boxes.

"Nic, we need to discuss this more," Becky charged.

The click from Nicholas unsnapping a fastener on one of the boxes was his only response.

"Nic!"

Abigail stood like a statue, her hands clasped tightly and body erect. Her eyes were darting back and forth between her parents.

The first box he opened contained a Smith & Wesson model 649, a small composite J-frame revolver, and nickel in color. He opened the cylinder and spun it.

Turning around, he said, "Abby, I think this will be the best one for you to have."

"I've shot that before, I think," she said.

Becky stepped up to Nicholas; only inches separated them. "Stop it."

"Please, Becky; I have to leave soon to go check on your parents. I don't know what will happen to me once I leave. I may not come back."

"Stop being so dramatic."

"I'm not, something bad has happened, and I believe it won't take long for people to go crazy."

"I think this outage is strange, but I can't imagine the world falling apart that quickly," Becky challenged.

"I can't afford to be wrong. Listen, I've taken her to the range before. She knows the basics and then some. Abby is a responsible young woman; she'll be fine."

"I'll be fine, Mom."

"She's a girl."

"You're not going to give up, are you?" Nicholas snapped.

"No, I'm putting my foot down. I let you do pretty much what you want, but when it comes to her, that's my territory."

His blood was boiling; his face had turned flush. A tingling sensation was covering his entire body. "Here's what we're going to do."

"Dad, don't back down," Abigail pleaded.

"It's important that parents talk. Your mother is correct, and we obviously need more time. Here's my compromise, you both come with me to your parents, along the way you can see for yourself what's happening out there, and if you're not convinced that Abby and you need to start having a gun close by, then you'll win, but only for a week. We will keep reassessing the situation."

"Dad!"

Becky thought and couldn't find a way to challenge his compromise. "Fine, when are we leaving?"

San Felipe, Mexico

Sleep was what Michael needed if he was going to have his

strength to escape, and it's what he made sure he got.

The rumble of a heavy exhaust woke him. He stumbled out of bed and walked to the window. By the light of the day, he had only gotten a couple hours of sleep.

In the driveway he saw two vehicles, one was Jose's Datsun truck and the other looked like an old Chevy Chevette. It had been tricked out with a spoiler, chrome wheels, and dual exhaust, but the neon purple color put it over the top in the category of ridiculous.

Jose's wife stepped out of the Chevette, and together as a family they walked into the house.

Michael could hear them talking with Marco; then silence for a minute was followed by a tap on his door. He sat on the bed, waiting for who might be coming into the room.

Jose stood with a toothy grin on his face.

"Good afternoon, Jose."

"*Buenas tardes, mi amigo.*"

"Why are you being so nice to me?" Michael asked. He had to know why this stranger would take care of him.

"The good Lord tells us to help others."

"You seem like a good man; you have a nice little family. How are you mixed up with these people?"

"What's the American saying? 'The tangled webs we weave'," Jose said.

"I don't see it, these guys are thugs. I don't see that in you."

Jose stepped farther into the room. "I needed help, and they needed something from me. It was a simple transaction. Now my girl is healthy, but I'm still paying that debt."

"Hmm, I see they have you by the balls, and once they do, there's no letting go."

"Something like that."

"I like the souped-up Chevette. I don't think I've seen one of those in years."

"You like it? Yes, I've been working on that for a couple of years. Thought I should bring it home. There's a shortage of cars that work."

"What are they saying about this outage? Is it affecting all of Mexico?" Michael asked.

"No, just the northern states. Most of Mexico is fine, but the United States did not make out so good. I heard some cities were nuked, your government is gone."

Michael tensed up and asked, "Nuked? Do they know who did it?"

"Russia, but it seems America hit them first after this grid attack."

"Where did you come by this information?"

"Mexican army is moving up here to provide support. I've heard from people talking to them. So, how's the memory?"

"Actually it's—I'm sorry I can't get past what you just told me."

"I'm sorry; it seems the world is falling apart."

Michael rubbed his head, confused by the recent news and unsure of his involvement in it.

"Your memory, not so good still, huh?" Jose said loudly enough for Marco to hear while holding up his hand for Michael to be quiet.

Understanding what he meant, Michael stopped talking.

"My friend, my beautiful wife is making a special dinner tonight. I want to invite you to dine with us at our table. Are you healthy enough to do that?" Jose asked, nodding his head.

"Yes, I'd like that."

"Good, dinner's in a couple hours. I'll come get you then," Jose said and immediately left the room, closing the door behind him.

Michael looked at the door and couldn't quite figure out Jose. On the outside he seemed like a simple man, a nice man, but there was a little edge and understanding of street culture that was coming through. He sensed there was something about to go down but couldn't quite put his finger on it.

Maybe tonight at dinner he'd understand better. Until then he would try to reclaim more of his memory.

Carlsbad, CA

Nicholas didn't want to encounter trouble along the way to his in-laws, but at the same time he wanted to prove to Becky that his theory of how society would treat the circumstances they were encountering was sound.

It took only five miles before his theory was showcased. He decided to take a drive by Albertson's grocery store, and there in stark relief was society doing exactly what he said they would.

The parking lot of the store was half full of cars, their hoods popped open. The front doors of the store were smashed, and people were coming out with carts full of food. Like a column of ants on a piece of food, they moved rapidly and irrespective of others.

Nicholas slowed down so she could get a good look.

"Why are those people looting? This is a good neighborhood," Becky said, her mouth open in astonishment of seeing it for herself. Scenes like this were something she had only witnessed on the news and happening in *other* towns or cities.

"Is this going to be another I-told-you-so moment?" Nicholas chided.

"Look, look," Abigail yelled.

"What?" Nicolas asked.

"Dad, look out!" Abigail screamed.

Nicholas looked up but didn't see anything, but his peripheral vision caught movement to his left.

Two men with bats came charging from the opposite side of the street.

Nicholas hit the accelerator, but an abandoned car was in his lane with only twenty feet between them. With a white-knuckled grip on the steering wheel, he jerked the car away from the men and onto the sidewalk.

Both Becky and Abigail screamed.

"Hold on!" Nicholas ordered as he drove the car down the sidewalk as far as he could before turning back onto the road.

In his rearview mirror he saw the men sprinting, but it

was impossible for them to catch them.

Abigail turned and was looking out the rear window, her pulse racing.

He made a right turn and slammed down on the accelerator. Clear of the trouble, he slowed down and turned to Becky, "You all right?"

Her eyes were wide and her breathing was rapid.

"I'm good, Dad," Abigail said. She then began to laugh.

"What's so funny?" Becky asked.

"Nothing, no everything, this is some crazy shit!" Abigail exclaimed.

"Now you're cursing?" Becky chastised.

"Well, Becky, how do you feel now?" Nicholas asked.

Combinations of conflicting emotions were colliding inside Becky. What she just experienced and what her eyes were feasting on made her feel uneasy, but she also wanted deep down to believe that it was nothing more than an aberration.

"I don't want to talk. Let's get to my parents' place."

Nicholas respected her feelings and didn't want to add to her stress. After what happened, he felt that his world view was validated. He applied pressure to the accelerator and sped off.

"Mom, Dad, you need to listen to me and Nic. It's going crazy out there, and you need to come with us," Becky pleaded.

"Frank, I think we need to listen to them," Marjory

said.

Chewing his food diligently, Frank didn't look up from his sandwich.

"Dad, are you listening to me?" Becky asked.

Nicholas stood against the far counter, his arms crossed and a slight crooked grin on his face. As if he needed more complications to his plan for bugging out, he had Frank to cause problems and put his plans and family in jeopardy.

"Becky, sweetheart, like I told your husband yesterday, we'll be fine. The government will get the power back up, and all this stuff will be forgotten in a couple weeks," Frank said, his mouth full of egg salad.

"But, Dad, I saw the craziness going on with my own eyes. People are not taking this well, and if the police or government can't respond accordingly, we will be on our own," Becky fired back.

"Nic, did you stop by Auto Zone yesterday for me?" Frank asked.

"Yeah, but they were closed," Nicholas said. Clearly he was lying.

"I'll need the car back soon. I need to go to the store soon," Frank said, his mind numbingly not grasping the severity of the problem.

"See, Becky, this is what I told you," Nicholas said, shaking his head in disgust at Frank's utter contempt.

"Dad, come with us, just for a drive. I'll show you the craziness going on," Becky said.

"I believe people are acting stupid. It's these younger generations, the entitlement babies."

"It's more than that," Becky said. After her brief but convincing encounter outside Albertson's, she was an advocate for Nicholas' plan to bug out.

"You're wasting your breath. They're not coming," Nicholas whispered to Becky.

"Nana, Papa, please listen to my dad. He knows what he's talking about," Abigail offered.

Frank turned to her and said, "My dear child, even if your father is right, we've had this conversation before. If this world has come to an end, I don't want to live in it. I don't want to survive. I'm too old for that and so is Marjory."

"Let Mom speak for herself, this once," Becky blurted out.

Frank cut Marjory a threatening look.

"I do what your father does," Marjory said.

For the second time that day Becky found herself arguing with a family member and not winning. Frustrated, she threw her arms in the air and walked out of the kitchen.

Marjory was clearly nervous. She fidgeted with her apron and kept messing with her gray hair.

Frank went back to eating his sandwich, his attention on a book.

Knowing this entire exercise was a waste of time, Nicholas left the kitchen to find Becky. He found her staring out the patio sliding door.

"I'm sorry," he said.

She wiped tears away and said, "No need to apologize. He's always been like that. Don't ask me why I care, but I do."

Nicholas never liked seeing her cry; he came up behind her and wrapped his arms around her.

"I'm sorry we fought earlier," Becky said. She held his arms tightly.

"Now there you go apologizing. This is all so strange for us. I don't know how to act either, who does?"

"I'm scared. We need to leave as soon as we can," Becky said.

"I can't take their car. I need to find another one. Exactly how I'm going to do that is a mystery."

"Just go to a car dealership."

"Ha, I don't think any are open."

"I'm serious, go to a car dealership and take one. I'm giving you permission to do what you have to do to take care of the family. We can't be bickering or fighting; we need to work together. I trust you. You've taken care of us this long; I need you to keep doing it."

"I never thought about going to a used-car dealership," Nicholas said. His mind was spinning on where to go. Unfortunately for him, the only places he knew that had older make cars were closer to downtown, and he was sure Becky's idea wasn't unique. If he was going to commit to their survival, he needed to go all the way. He needed another car, but just as important, he needed to get other like-minded people on his side.

San Diego, CA

When the sun set on the second day, Bryn, Sophie and Matt had gone back to the Best Buy and taken away more water, the remaining food and batteries. Bryn felt very proud of what they had accomplished, but she knew the easier days would end soon. She felt deep down that they would not be able to survive within the city limits for too long.

"I'm so tired," Matt said, exhaling loudly as he stretched out on Bryn's apartment floor.

"I am too," Sophie added.

Bryn was busy admiring the food and stacks of bottled water they had gotten during their scavenging.

"Do you suppose we'll get in trouble for all of this?" Sophie asked them.

"From who?" Bryn asked.

"I haven't seen one cop, not one, not any firemen, nothing," Matt said.

"Yeah, where's the military? Why aren't they doing something?" Sophie asked.

"Well, Matt says these types of things can affect everything and everyone. So it only gives more credence that your theory is correct, and if it is, then no one is coming to help us," Bryn said as she turned and faced the other two.

"So, this is it? This is the end of the world? I can't believe it," Sophie said as she plopped onto the couch.

"And no zombies, I'm kinda bummed," Matt joked.

"I could never get into the zombie stuff," Sophie responded.

"I love anything post-apocalyptic or dystopian, and there' so much cool stuff out there," Matt said.

"Well, now you're living it," Bryn chimed in.

"I wonder if this is happening everywhere. I can't believe it would be," Sophie added.

"We need to plan like it is," Bryn answered.

"But someone sometime is going to come and help us. I just refuse to think that this is it; it can't be."

"Logically, I agree, but Bryn is right, we don't know how long we will all be here waiting," Matt said, sitting up.

"How do you suppose Mom is doing?" Sophie asked.

Bryn chose to ignore her.

"You said your mom lives in La Jolla, whereabouts?" Matt asked.

"She has this great place near the top of Mount Soledad. It's so beautiful, has awesome views of the ocean. God, I miss my bedroom there. I swear that's the most comfortable bed."

"Why don't we go there?" Matt asked the obvious.

"We're not going anywhere," Bryn barked.

"Why not? If we have to sit and wait for help to come, that seems like a better place to do it. How long before we get into a fight with the idiots outside?" Sophie said.

"I'm not going to Mom's, period," Bryn exclaimed.

Matt watched the sisters argue. Clearly there was a much deeper meaning to why Bryn didn't have a desire to go to her mom's, whose house couldn't be more than four or five miles away.

"If she lives in the Soledad area, that's an easy walk. We could ferry our stuff there," Matt said.

"I agree with Matt. Let's go to Mom's," Sophie said.

"We don't need her. We can make do here," Bryn again barked, digging in her heels.

"What is your deal? You really need to move on, Bryn!" Sophie charged.

"I don't *need* to do anything!" Bryn shot back.

"It does make sense to go to a nice area and be in a house," Matt added.

"If you two want to go, you can. I'm staying put," Bryn fired.

"Don't be like that," Sophie pleaded.

Bryn calmed down and walked over to Sophie. "Baby sister, I won't be going to Mom's house, and that's my final answer."

Sophie shook her head, frustrated by Bryn's resistance and stubborn resolve.

Bryn said, "You two stay here. I'll be back shortly." She quickly got up and headed for the door.

"Where you going?" Sophie asked.

"The old man has something that we can use. I shouldn't be gone longer than a couple of hours," she said, then closed the door.

When the door shut, Matt asked, "What's the deal with her and your mom?"

"She blames Mom for what happened to Dad. And Mom wasn't the best mother while we were growing up, but I've moved past all that. I don't believe in living in the past. Bryn, though, can't move on. When she holds a grudge, watch out, she'll never let it go."

"I'll keep that in mind," Matt joked and relaxed back on the floor. His body was sore from the miles walked.

"Do you really think we need to plan for the worst?" Sophie asked.

"I'm only guessing at what this could be, but I've seen enough movies and read enough books to know that this has all the earmarks of the end. So, yes, we need to plan for the worst."

After Bryn closed the apartment door, she stood and listened. She could hear Sophie and Matt still talking, but she was listening for other sounds. Her dilated eyes peered into the darkness, but gone were the lights she was so accustomed to seeing. Without the light, she needed to perfect her other senses, so with intentional focus she listened carefully to the sounds of the evening. Slowly things came to her. Somewhere in the far distance she heard a car driving, a baby crying somewhere in her complex then hit her ears, followed by some yelling, which was familiar as it was a neighbor who lived several buildings away. Then other noises and sounds came, a random series of gunshots cracked far away, then a dog barking, doors opening, slamming. She reached out and grasped the railing and leaned out, her eyes now adjusting to the darkness.

Her ears then began to work in tandem with her eyes as she heard then spotted the dark shadow moving through the parking lot. The person stopped, but she couldn't tell what they were doing, then a light appeared. The person was holding a flashlight. The long beam stretched out far beyond and illuminated the darkness. The person was going from car to car, looking inside.

She knew this person was looking to scavenge. At first she had an impulse to yell out, but she stopped. How was this person any different than her? She had been stealing since yesterday, so how could she tell this person not to? Questions filled her mind, "Was there a code to theft?" "Did it matter where or who you stole from?" The questions were foreign to her, but deep down trying to steal from her neighbors did seem wrong. She knew that didn't make sense, but to her it did. If this person were out on the road, she wouldn't think twice, but since they were looking through her neighbors cars, it did seem wrong.

Going with her gut, a sense she would rely upon heavily in this new world, she cried out, "Hey, what are you doing?"

The light stopped and flashed in her direction, but she quickly knelt down, taking cover behind the railing. The light darted back and forth, but Bryn stayed put, out of sight. Eventually, the light disappeared, and she heard the footsteps of the unknown person quickly walk away.

She stood, smiled to herself, and made for Colin's apartment.

Unsure of the time, she assumed he'd be awake, but regardless she wanted his help if he was willing to do it.

She knocked and waited, a minute went by but nothing. She knocked again and this time she got a response.

"Who goes there?"

"Bryn, your neighbor."

The door opened quickly, the yellow glow of candles and a few kerosene lanterns burst out and cast upon her tanned skin, soiled jeans and T-shirt.

"You came. Wasn't sure if you were going to make it," Colin said, his eyes then looked past her. "Anyone with you?"

"Nope, just me."

"Come on in," he said and opened the door fully.

A strong whiff of fragrance hit her as she stepped into his apartment. She took another sniff and recognized the smell, pine. Somewhere among the few candles he had lit was a pine-scented candle. The smell reminded her of Christmas and with it brought memories, not all good.

"Where are the other two?"

"Back at my place, I thought it best I come alone."

"Take a seat; can I get you a drink, water, beer or whiskey?"

Bryn was tempted to have a drink, but she wanted to focus. This wasn't a social call. "Water would be fine."

Colin disappeared into the kitchen and re-emerged with a glass. He handed it to her and said, "Here ya go."

"Thanks," Bryn responded as she looked at the glass. She didn't get a vibe from him, but her guard was up when she saw the glass. She didn't think he'd slip her something, but she just couldn't trust anyone. She placed the glass down on the coffee table in front of her.

The apartment was the exact same floor plan as hers.

The front door opened to a small living room on the left, dining space on the right and kitchen in the right corner. A hallway straight ahead led to a single bathroom and the single bedroom at the end. However, the similarities ended with the floor plan. Colin's décor was lacking as Bryn looked around. She wasn't one who prided herself on being on the cutting edge of interior design; her style would be characterized as more of a minimalist. Colin was clearly the opposite. Everywhere there could be a piece of furniture, there was, and on it was stacked items. The coffee table in front of her was loaded with magazines and knickknack items. Looking at him, she never would have thought he was a collector of such things, but here was his apartment the telltale of a part of him. The walls also showed the same abundance of items. Above her head, there was barely an inch of wall showing in between the framed pictures and military awards. Colin couldn't be called a hoarder, but he definitely had an issue with getting rid of things.

"So you were some sort of military guy?" Bryn asked as she saw many pictures of him in uniform.

"Yeah, I was in the Navy," he answered and sat down himself, across from her in an old fabric recliner, a glass of water in his hands.

Bryn was nervous and wanted to get to the point of her visit but thought it proper to have meaningless dialogue beforehand.

"Did you go to war?"

Colin knew she was anxious and only asking to pass the time. In an attempt to relieve her of this stress, he went right into why she was there. "You need a gun?"

"Yes."

"One second." He stood and left the room.

She heard some rustling and other noises, and within moments he reappeared holding a box. He placed it on the table and opened it up. She was curious as to what he had, so she leaned forward.

The light in the room wasn't bright even after her eyes had adjusted.

"What you need if you're going to be running around is something compact. You can't go around carrying a shotgun. This little piece will come in handy for you," he said, handing her a small revolver, the cylinder open.

She took it in her hand and was amazed by how light it was. "What is it?"

"It's an old Colt Detective model. It's lightweight, and this little guy has an advantage over other smaller revolvers, it carries six not five."

She admired it while also feeling let down. She had hoped to get a pistol like she'd seen in movies. "I really don't mean to be ungrateful, but do you have something bigger and..." She paused, trying to find the words to describe what she had envisioned.

"That size is perfect for you."

"Um, anything black and has the thing that goes back and forth up here," she remarked.

"You want a semi-auto pistol?"

"Yes, that's it."

"Have you ever shot a gun before?"

Bryn didn't want to answer, but she knew she had to and do it honestly, "No, never."

"Then without proper training, this is the piece for you."

"What's to learn? You just point and shoot."

"Ha, if only it were so easy." Colin laughed.

She closed the cylinder and held it tightly in her hand. These were not times to act like you knew everything. If she was going to survive, she needed to learn, and he was the guy who could help her. "Teach me how to use this."

"I can do that."

"What's it going to cost me, though?"

"Nothing, nothing at all."

"Nothing?"

"I just like helping."

"Everything has a price," she challenged.

"I have plenty, and you seem like a good girl. I like helping people, been in my blood since I joined the Navy years ago. I was given a second chance at life, and whenever I can pass it forward, I do."

"I insist, let me pay you something."

"No, really, it's not necessary."

"Something."

"If you insist, I'll take a case of that water, nothing more."

Bryn thought she could sense he was just as stubborn as her. "Deal."

San Felipe, Mexico

Dinner was much later than he had been promised. Michael didn't care. When he ate didn't matter; what he was more interested in was what he thought might be happening.

"Michael, I never formally introduced you to my wife. This is Francesca. Isn't she a beauty? You already know my two little ones, Maria and Jose, but we call him Junior."

"Nice to meet you. Thank you again for taking such good care of me."

Marco sat at the head of the table, his bulky frame dwarfing the table and Michael, who sat next to him.

Francesca smiled broadly and said, "Welcome to our table. I hope you enjoy what I've prepared."

"It smells wonderful," Michael said. He was grateful that the swelling had gone down enough that he could now see out of both eyes.

Marco just sat emotionless and grunted when asked if he liked carnitas.

With the food dished out and before anyone could dig in, Jose spoke. "If everyone could bow their heads for a prayer."

Michael obliged and with his good eye winked at little Maria, who wouldn't stop looking and smiling at him.

Jose recited the standard Catholic meal prayer and then finished off with a toast. With the formalities behind them, everyone dug into their plates and began eating.

Michael's memory of his past had essentially come back, but any recollection of what he was doing on the ship and who might have launched the nuclear missile was still unavailable to him.

Consumed with eating, Marco stopped his relentless staring at Michael. As if he hadn't eaten in weeks, the large man ate with ferocity. Michael wondered if he was man or animal.

Junior and Maria were laughing to themselves at how Marco conducted himself at the table.

"Where are you from, Michael?" Jose asked.

Almost taking the bait, Michael caught himself and said, "I wish I could tell you, but I don't remember."

"If you don't remember anything, how can you speak?" Marco blurted out, food falling from his overstuffed mouth.

"I don't understand," Michael answered.

"Your memory, how do you know how to speak? Why don't you forget how to speak?"

"Hmm, good question. I don't know," Michael said.

"Amnesia is a common thing after an injury to the head," Jose interjected. He looked at Marco and saw he needed more beer. *"Mas cerveza?"*

"Si," Marco answered him.

Jose looked at his wife and nodded.

She left the room.

"I think you're lying, but it doesn't matter whether I take you over there tomorrow or in a week, you're going to speak. The boss won't waste too much time and then you'll be mine, gringo."

Michael raised his eyebrows and swallowed hard. He knew what that meant. Grabbing his napkin, he wiped his lips. When he put it back on his lap, he pulled the glass shank from his pocket and tucked it under his leg.

"Miguel, I can promise you, I don't remember anything," Michael cracked.

"Marco, my name is Marco."

"Sorry, see, I can't even remember your name."

Marco stared at him hard and grunted. "Funny, gringo, I'll be having the last laugh."

Francesca came back in the room and placed a beer in front of Marco.

He picked it up and swigged half the bottle down.

"Can I get you more food?" Francesca asked.

"I'm fine," Michael said.

"She was asking me, gringo!" Marco said, slamming his beer down.

The children jumped and looked scared.

"Please take them to their rooms. It's time for bed," Jose ordered Francesca.

Quickly she gathered them up and left.

As the awkward seconds turned to minutes, Michael could sense his moment might be coming. He placed his right hand on his lap and readied himself.

Jose opened his mouth to talk, but Marco cut him off. "You must think handing this gringo over will get you some leniency, don't you, Jose?"

"I'm just being a loyal servant is all," Jose answered.

"What exactly was wrong with your girl?" Michael asked.

"Cancer, we couldn't get the care we needed here, so Manuel lent me the money and got us across the border so she could get the treatment she needed. That was last year, and now she's in remission. God blessed us."

"God? More like the boss blessed you. You and your fucking God," Marco exclaimed boldly.

Jose looked at his empty plate and fiddled with his fork.

Marco finished his beer and slammed the bottle on the table. "I want another."

"I'll get it," Jose said and stood up.

"No, have the gringo get it," Marco ordered.

"It's okay; I'm closer to the kitchen," Jose said and turned to leave.

"No!" Marco yelled, slamming his fist into the table. "The gringo gets it!"

Michael was nervous about standing; the shank was underneath his leg. If he stood too quickly, it might fall on the floor, but how could he put it back in his pocket without Marco seeing it.

"Get me a fucking beer, white boy!" Marco barked.

Michael swallowed hard. A bead of sweat coursed down his temple and a nervous flutter hit his stomach.

"Are you deaf?" Marco asked Michael as he waited for him to get up.

"No, I can hear you just fine," Michael replied and slowly stood up, trying not to move the shank, but the tip snagged on his pants and he pulled it off the chair. It hit the floor with a thud.

Marco looked down. His eyes grew two sizes when he saw what it was.

Michael also looked at the shank lying on the floor. He

wanted to grab it, but would he be quick enough?

Their eyes met, but no one moved. Both stood frozen, like a game of chicken, who would move first?

Marco leapt from his chair and tackled Michael. As he fell to the floor with Marco's mass on top of him, Michael took the moment to think about how fast he was for such a large man. He would never have guessed he would be so spry.

Marco began pummeling Michael in the face with his fists, one punch after another.

Michael reached up and jammed his right thumb into Marco's left eye and punched him in the neck with his left.

Marco recoiled from the eye jam and throat punch, but almost immediately composed himself and went back to battering Michael.

Michael threw every combination of punch he knew, but Marco was unstoppable.

As one punch after another connected with Michael's already injured head, he began to feel himself slipping away.

Suddenly Marco yelped and fell off of him.

Michael looked and saw Marco squirming on the floor next to him.

Above him was Jose. He held a large ten-inch culinary knife in his right hand. He raised it and came down with a forceful blow into Marco's chest this time.

Marco yelled out.

Again, Jose plunged the blade into Marco.

Seeing his opportunity, Michael grabbed Marco and put him in a head lock and began to apply pressure on his thick neck.

This choke hold exposed Marco's chest and gave Jose an unobstructed target for the knife and he took it. Three more times he came down with a ferocity that few men are capable of.

Like a bull, Michael held on as Marco's massive body shifted and squirmed in a feeble attempt to free himself from Michael's hold, but the repeated knife blows to the chest weakened him.

What felt like an eternity was probably no more than a minute as Michael clamped down until Marco stopped moving. Michael released him and scurried out from underneath him and sat up.

Blood freely poured out of the half a dozen two-inch knife wounds soaking Marco's white shirt.

Michael was shocked at Jose's barbarity; it wasn't something he thought the man was capable of.

Panting heavily, Jose looked at Marco then turned to Michael.

This look gave Michael pause as he wondered if he was Jose's next target.

Jose looked at the bloody knife; his face cringed as he tossed the knife on the floor.

"Thank you," Michael said.

"He was an evil man, pure evil," Jose muttered.

"I can't thank you enough for everything," Michael said, the fight with Marco taking a toll on his already battered body.

A loud banging on the front door startled both men.

Michael looked at the door then at Jose.

Jose said, "We have to leave, now." He turned and ran

for the hallway.

Michael saw exactly what he needed just then, a pistol. He pulled it out of Marco's shoulder holster and press-checked it. He scrambled to the opposite wall and contemplated his next move.

Loud knocks turned to kicking and banging. The yells and chatter were unintelligible, but Michael knew it was Marco's colleagues.

Using the wall, he eased up till he was standing. With a firm grip on the Beretta 9mm, he patiently waited for them to enter.

With explosive force the door burst open, pieces of splintered wood flew, and the door hung from one hinge.

Manuel and two of his men came in, pistols in their hands.

"Marco!" Manuel yelled.

Attempting to ease his rapid heart rate, Michael took several long and slow breaths. His ears listened intently for where the men were.

A child's cry came from the hall.

"Marco, where are you?" Manuel called out.

Michael could hear they were in the front room but not moving closer.

Under his breath he mumbled, "C'mon, motherfuckers."

"Marco!" Manuel again called out.

Michael knew they were being cautious, so if they weren't coming to him, he'd have to go to them. Carefully he stepped to where the dining room wall met the short hallway that led to the foyer and front living room. Once there, his ears picked up on what sounded like three men discussing their options in Spanish. They stopped talking and the sound Michael wanted to hear came; the creaking of feet walking down the hall hit his ears.

He pressed his eyes shut, said a quick prayer and pivoted around the corner. There he saw all three men stacked up walking slowly. Michael instantly squeezed off the first round, hitting the first man. Not wasting time, he put the sights on the second and again squeezed off a round. The bullet hit that man in the chest.

He grunted and fell to the ground dead.

With two men down, Michael turned the sights on the third man, Manuel. However, his success ended there.

Manuel leveled his handgun and fired several times; all three bullets missed Michael but forced him to take cover.

"I see you. You can't escape, American, just know that," Manuel hollered.

"It's just you and me. I can promise you that I'll be the last man standing," Michael responded arrogantly.

"I don't think so."

"I remembered everything, and let me say, you're fucking with the wrong guy."

The entire time they talked to each other, Manuel crept back towards the front door.

"I'll come back for you, American, I will," Manuel yelled. He turned and ran out the front towards his vehicle.

Hearing this, Michael pursued him, but when he exited, Manuel repelled his advance with a volley of bullets. Michael took cover and waited.

Safely now in his vehicle, Manuel started it and left.

Knowing his time to leave was limited; Michael picked up the weapons from the dead men and found Jose with his family cowering in the back bedroom.

"I hope you don't mind, but I'm taking one of those cars you have," Michael said.

"Take the Chevette. That's why I brought it back."

"I don't know how to thank you," Michael replied.

"No thanks, I did this for selfish reasons too. Saving you saved me. I needed to do a good deed like this to be forgiven for the horrible things I've been made to do by these disgusting men and Manuel," Jose said and spit on the floor.

"Are you safe here?"

"We're leaving too. There's nothing here for us. We have family in Loreto; we're heading there."

Jose walked Michael out to the car. He gave him the keys and asked, "Did you have something to do with the missile?"

His memory was still a blank, but there wasn't any doubt he had some part in it. He needed to go find the one person who might be able to help him remember who he was; that person was his brother, Nicholas. "I think so."

"Where will you go?"

"I'm headed to San Diego."

Carlsbad, CA

The last person Nicholas wanted to see was Brent, but

there he was standing on the edge of his driveway and the street, looking at them as they pulled into their garage. What most worried Nicholas was he wasn't alone. Alongside him were Chandler Nolte, the HOA president; Geraldine Francis, HOA board member; and two other people he'd never met.

"How soon before that piece of shit shows up asking for a lift?" Nicholas asked.

"What's Chandler doing here?" Becky asked.

While Nicholas pulled up the heavy wood-sided garage door, all eyes were on him and his car. Swiftly he put the car inside and closed the door.

"Can we leave now?" Nicholas asked.

"Not until you get another car," Becky answered him as she navigated through the darkness around boxes and equipment.

"I knew you were going to say that," Nicholas fretted.

"There's no other choice. Just get it done. I'll organize our things. As soon as you have it, we can leave."

Nicholas needed help, and the best place he thought about finding it was with his good friend Proctor Simmons. Over the past year and a half, Nicholas had confided his belief that things could come to an end. Proctor heard him clearly and also began to prepare, but like Nicholas hadn't gotten all he needed. Nicholas would drive to his house tomorrow and enlist him for his cause. Proctor had assets, but the skill set he had above others was he was a medically trained doctor. An ob-gyn by trade, his overall medical training could be critical, plus he had an office that surely had medical supplies, something Nicholas had but not in abundance.

"When are you leaving?" Becky asked.

"Not until tomorrow morning, it's safer, I think. I can at least see when someone's coming at me."

"Makes sense."

They both began to chat more when a loud bang at the door echoed throughout the house.

"Guess who?" Nicholas quipped. He made his way to the front door, with Becky just a few feet behind him.

When he opened the heavy eight-foot-tall door, he found exactly who he thought he'd find, Brent, Chandler, Geraldine and the two other people.

"Brent, Chandler, Gerry, nice to see you all," Nicholas said.

"Hi, Nic," Brent said, a stern look etched on his face. His jaws were clenched and his brow furrowed.

"What can I do for you?" Nicholas asked.

"Sorry, do you want to come in?" Becky interjected.

Nicholas gave Becky a blank stare, which told her everything about what she just did. He opened the door wide and motioned with his arm for them to enter.

One by one his unwelcome neighbors stepped across his threshold.

Becky exited the room and returned a minute later with two lanterns. She set them in a large seating area next to the foyer. The LED lights gave off a warm white glow and created an odd atmosphere.

The seating arrangements made Nicholas feel this was a tribunal. His guests sat across from him while he and Becky sat opposite in a small love seat.

"So sorry for interrupting you, but Brent brought something to our attention that we wanted to address with you," Chandler said. He was a tall and sturdy man. He stood over six feet four inches, and the rumors were he left his career as a professional football player after being implicated in a gambling racket. He vehemently denied those rumors and the NFL never found solid evidence, but those rumors were enough to make a mediocre quarterback toxic, and within three years of going from team to team, he finished his career as a San Diego Charger.

"Let me guess, the car," Nicholas responded.

"Yes, that's it. Nicholas, we don't know what's happening, but no one's cars are working and our attempts to contact EMS have not worked out. It's not that we didn't try. Several of our neighbors walked to the closest fire station, but they found three firemen with no answers, and none of their vehicles were working. Needless to say, it was disheartening."

"You want to use the car I have?"

"Why did you lie to me?" Brent asked with a sharp tone.

"I didn't lie. When you stopped by the first day, I didn't have it then. I picked it up later from my father-in-law."

"I asked you to let me know, but you didn't. I told you my son needs his prescriptions," Brent chided.

"Sorry, Brent, let's just say you're not high on my list to help. I seem to remember you dimed me out after that party."

"You can't get over that, can you?"

"Who would, and who does that to their neighbor? We weren't having a kegger, just a party, and yes, some people got a bit excited, but we weren't having a goddamn rave."

"Chandler, do something," Brent ordered.

"Brent, Nicholas, please stop your bickering. Our community has an emergency and we need to come together. Nicholas, you have a car that works, and we have neighbors in need. I don't have any right to dictate what you can do with your car, but I can ask on behalf of the community. Can you allow us access to your car to go procure food, water and other essential items?"

Nicholas didn't answer. He sat staring at the lantern. He hated being put in the situation he just found himself in. It wasn't that he didn't want to contribute; he just didn't put his neighbors as a priority. For him, his family was that, but how could he say no to them. Of course, in theory, declining to help was easy, but how do you do it when those people are sitting right in front of you.

"Nic?" Chandler asked.

Becky also noticed the awkward pause and touched his knee.

"Thoughts?" Nicholas asked Becky.

Her response was a simple nod.

"Chandler, I will do what I can, but let it be known I can't make guarantees that I'll be able to get everything for everyone. What I recommend is we get a few in the neighborhood to come with me and look for more cars. This seems like the practical first step towards equipping you with the tools you'll need to get past this emergency."

"Until the authorities can fix this, yes, that makes

sense," Chandler inserted.

"Good, I'm leaving in the morning; put together a list of items needed and give me two capable people to join me. And when I say capable, I mean ready to fight if need be, I want them armed. If you know someone in the community who knows how to hot-wire a car that would be beneficial too."

"Armed?" Geraldine asked. Her face showed concern.

"Yes, armed, I've been out there twice, and things are starting to deteriorate. We were attacked earlier today. It's only going to get worse, and where we have to go tomorrow, I'm betting we might encounter some trouble."

"I'm coming with you," Brent said.

"Do you have a gun?" Nicholas asked.

"No, but I can handle myself," Brent answered as he sat straighter in his chair.

"Do you know how to handle a gun?" Nicholas asked.

"No, I mean yes, I shot a .22 rifle when I was a kid."

Nicholas exhaled loudly.

"Is this really a critical requirement?" Chandler asked.

"I have the car, I set the requirements," Nicholas stated.

"This is bullshit!" Brent barked.

"Chandler, please have two capable men and a list. Please prioritize the items, medicine at the top," Nicholas said.

"I will. When do you need it by?"

"Early, say five thirty tomorrow morning. I'll need to review the list and make a route."

"I'll have it here by then. Thank you. Does anyone

have anything to add?" Chandler asked.

Everyone sat silent.

Brent was stewing, his jaw clenched and brows pressed together tightly as he kept staring at Nicholas.

Nicholas escorted them out and stopped Chandler just before he exited. "Hey, listen. I won't have the car long; also you need to begin organizing things."

"Is that something you'd like to help with?"

"Can't, we're leaving."

"Leaving? Where are you going?"

"Somewhere safer, I hope," Nicholas confided.

"Well, let's hope this passes over quickly. Most people don't have a lot of food, and those that have ventured out said things are getting a bit crazy out there. We need this to go well tomorrow," Chandler said and patted Nicholas' shoulder. He walked out and into the darkness.

After closing the door, Nicholas turned to Becky and said, "Great, not that I didn't have enough to do, I have to run errands for our neighbors."

"Let's talk about it over dinner, and stop bellyaching. At least we have a car."

Abigail was sitting in the kitchen, writing in her journal. She looked up when they entered and asked, "Dad, here's the addresses for my friends. You promised to stop by and check on them."

"More errands?" Nicholas lamented.

"You promised," Abigail said and kissed him on the cheek. She grabbed a lantern and shuffled out of the kitchen.

He looked at the names. There were four listed; the top

had a star next to it. "Do you know a Rob Robles?"

"Who?"

"Rob Robles. I don't think I've met him before, have you?"

Becky was busy making dinner; her focus was on mixing the ingredients not listening to Nicholas. "Honey, can you grab those lanterns or light some candles? I can't see that well."

"Sure," he said and walked out to grab the ones in the front seating room. "Hmm, Rob Robles, are you what I think you might be?"

San Diego, CA

With an agreement struck, Colin finished the evening by giving Bryn the basics of marksmanship. He started by detailing the nomenclature of the revolver and the simple functionality behind it. He stressed that its simple mechanisms made it the perfect piece for her until she had further training and education. She attempted to argue with him that she needed the semi-auto, but he refused by telling her that not knowing how to operate one could prove fatal.

"Malfunctions happen, and if you don't have the training, it could be the last thing you do. What is beautiful about a revolver is that a simple misfire doesn't require much but squeezing the trigger again."

He covered more detail with her and eventually he showed her tactical stances and movements. He went over how to quickly reload the revolver and stressed the importance of only firing when she had a target. The revolver had limited capacity, so she needed to make each shot count.

Neither paid attention to the time, so when Bryn looked at her watch, she was shocked to see how quickly the time had melted away.

"Oh my God, it's almost midnight."

"Time flies when you're having fun."

"When can I shoot this? I want to shoot this," Bryn said enthusiastically.

"Unfortunately, I think you'll get a chance to use it for defensive purposes sooner than you want."

That reality hit her as she looked at the handgun in her hands. A flood of emotions washed over her rapidly as she then thought of where she was just a week ago. How strange that everything had shifted and changed so much that now she was in her neighbor's apartment, holding a gun and getting tactical training.

"I don't recommend we go out shooting, so you'll have to just train by dry firing. That will get you used to the trigger pull and proper aiming."

"Can I take it with me?"

"Sure, you need it," he said, sliding the box over to her.

She looked inside to discover a box of fifty hollow-point bullets, three reloaders with cartridges and another smaller box that held a cleaning kit.

He walked back into his bedroom and came out holding something; he handed it to her and said, "You'll need this too."

She took and examined it.

"It's a small clip holster; it slides into your waistband. Use your shirt to conceal it."

She did what he said, tucked the holster in her pants and inserted the pistol. It fit snugly, and with it, she felt empowered.

"Oh, and take this too," he said, handing her a folding knife with clip.

Taking it, she slowly opened the blade. The knife looked intimidating with its serrated edge. "I can't thank you enough."

"Same time tomorrow, we'll do some more training, okay?" he asked.

"Same time tomorrow," she responded as she clipped the knife in her right pocket and walked to the door. She stopped herself short of opening it, turned and asked, "What do you think is going on?"

"Armageddon, I assume."

"No, what do you think happened?"

"Hell, I don't know. Does it matter now? Shit's not working, and when shit doesn't work, people go crazy."

"Crazy is right. It wasn't twelve hours and people were ransacking stores and hurting other people."

"People were doing that before, but on a much smaller scale. Keep that in mind."

"I guess you're right."

"Don't worry about the why. In fact, don't worry; plan, prepare and stay on your toes. What happened happened; that ship has sailed. If you want to see the sun rise for many more years, you're going to need to put the party girl in a box and get your game face on."

"Party girl?"

"You think I never saw you every weekend coming and going, drinking and partying? I know everything."

"Okay, now you're creeping me out. What? Have you been stalking me?"

"Ha, no, nothing like that. You just never noticed me. I've always been sitting on my perch, smoking cigars or having a drink. You were just too busy with your life and your smart phone to ever see me. So many people are now *seeing* for the first time, and it's scary. They woke up to a world that's not going back more than likely, and now that they can see, they know they're not ready. They never prepared, they never took the time to learn the skills that humans had learned for millennia. The knowledge of their inabilities is frightening."

"Makes sense. I know I was…am a bit scared, but I'm a quick study."

"I can see that," Colin said with a smile.

"Why did it all fall apart so quickly?"

"Because we were never really held together that tightly."

CHAPTER 3

"Those who fail to plan, plan to fail." – Alan Lakein

Carlsbad, CA

Nicholas again didn't wait for the sun. He was up at five and already in the garage, preparing for the day's adventure.

Siphoning gas from his Mercedes, he topped off the Dodge and filled an additional five-gallon can, which he stored in the trunk. Besides his preferred handgun, the Sig Sauer P239, he carried a second, the Sig Sauer P220, and also took a rifle, an AR-15.

The Marine Corps had given him much-needed skills and training, but he also left the Corps years ago with a half-dozen thirty-round magazines. These were banned in California, but now knowing that most law enforcement was out of commission, he loaded the magazines with glee, knowing he'd have the firepower to protect himself. Another item he fixed in the early morning hours was the 'bullet button' on his rifle. It didn't take a gunsmith to remove it and put in a proper magazine release. There was no way he was going into a possible gunfight with one arm tied behind his back.

With both he and the car ready for the day, all he needed now was the list and two more able-bodied men.

Right on time he heard footsteps coming his way in the predawn morning. A chilled breeze blew in from the west and the birds began to rise from their slumber. Again he marveled at how Mother Nature ignored the bane of humans and continued on. Even if mankind found a way to destroy itself, the planet would keep spinning and moving through space in its orbit around the sun. What nature told him was they weren't as important as they thought they were. Just because their world was falling apart didn't mean theirs had to as well.

Chandler and two men emerged from the shadows.

Nicholas didn't recognize the first man; he stepped up and introduced himself immediately.

"Nicholas, hello, my name is Alex. Nice to meet you." Alex was a man of average height and build. Nicholas guessed he was in his late thirties to early forties.

Just behind Alex was Brent.

"Chandler, what's he doing here?" Nicholas asked.

"He insisted on coming due to his son's prescription," Chandler answered, handing Nicholas a sheet of paper.

"You heard him, he doesn't own a gun. How can I rely on him out there?"

"I'm not going to get into this. Please let him go," Chandler begged.

"I've got a piece," Alex said, lifting up his shirt to show Nicholas a semiautomatic pistol.

"You know how to use it?" Nicholas asked.

"Ten years as a cop, and I know how to hot-wire a car."

"Aren't you a jack of all trades." Nicholas laughed.

"I had an interesting childhood, to say the least."

"Must have, I thought I knew a lot of stuff, but hot-wiring old cars was never on my list."

"I can also pick locks."

"Were you a cop or a con?" Nicholas joked.

"They say you have to be one to catch one," Alex said and winked at him.

"Good man, glad to have you here," Nicholas said as he turned on his headlamp to read the list. "Who the hell put ice on this? Fucking idiot."

"I put everything down like you asked," Chandler said defensively.

"Come on, Chandler. Ice, really? Oh, and dry cleaning? What the hell, man, I'm not a damn delivery service. I said only critical items." Nicholas took out a felt-tip marker and began to cross off items. "Gone, gone, nope, really, nope, no, no, no, I don't think so."

"You're marking off most of the list," Chandler moaned.

"Because most of the list is bullshit. I'm not picking up crayons. I don't think paper towels are critical, nor do I think risking my life for Purina Cat food is worth it, and all of this shit about organic food. Seriously, this might be the apocalypse; organic and non-GMO is not going to happen. They'll be begging for a can of fucking Spam after a couple weeks of starving."

"I'm just the messenger," Chandler responded.

Nicholas gathered them around the hood of the car and laid out a map. He pointed to the places they would go in order. He pointed to Proctor's house in Carmel Valley, approximately twelve miles south; from there they'd head directly for some car lots down in Pacific Beach he'd found in the phone book. If they were able to secure more vehicles, they'd convoy to get food and water. Nicholas ruled out grocery stores; that was the low-hanging fruit. Using the phone book he found a commercial kitchen in Claremont and a Sysco Food warehouse in Poway. He just couldn't imagine they had been hit up yet, so it was worth the drive. In total they'd be driving over fifty miles of potentially dangerous highways, roads and streets.

Everyone agreed to the route, with Brent staying oddly quiet.

Chandler wished them well and again thanked Nicholas.

When Nicholas pulled out of the driveway, he took a moment and stopped.

"What's up?" Alex asked.

Nicholas looked at his house. He smiled and said, "I just want to take a mental picture of it."

"Oh."

"You know, so I don't forget it," Nicholas added.

"You're freaking me out," Brent blurted out.

"I get it; I used to do that too when I was a cop. You never know if you're going to come home."

"Alex, you get me."

Disgruntled, Brent huffed and looked out the window.

Nicholas looked at Alex and turned to face Brent, who was sitting in the rear passenger-side seat. "As my dad used to say, let's keep our powder dry and always stay off the horizon."

He leveled his foot against the accelerator and sped off.

San Diego, CA

Bryn woke the second the sun made its appearance. She bolted out of bed and got dressed; making sure her new weapon was neatly on her person. She felt a high, a self-confidence that she hadn't felt just the day before. She fully knew that having a pistol and knife wouldn't keep her alive forever, but it helped. Her next goal was to find a vehicle. Not only would it come in handy for scavenging, but she knew that eventually they'd have to leave. To where, well, she wasn't sure just yet.

She walked into the living room to discover Matt and Sophie were positioned almost identical to how she found them upon her return earlier.

Matt was sprawled on the floor, snoring, and Sophie was curled up on her side, in an almost fetal position on the couch.

Bryn walked into the kitchen, opened a bottled water and tore into a bag of jerky. As she ate her skimpy breakfast, she charted her day. She wanted to keep gathering food and water, but with the small stockpile she and the others had gathered, she was nervous now about protecting that. Not only were the three amigos on her mind but whoever was lurking in the parking lot last night. They couldn't hide what they were doing, and she noticed that with each trip, more and more eyes were on them.

Soon those who weren't scavenging or didn't have food or water would be knocking on their door.

She walked over to Matt, his mouth wide open and his hand placed on his plump belly. Kicking him, she said, "Get up, new day."

Like the day before he shot up, his eyes wide. "What, huh?"

"We have a lot to do today. Get up," she answered him.

Bryn then went to Sophie, but she didn't have to wake her. Sophie rolled over and said, "I'm awake. Where to today?"

"I love your enthusiasm, little sis." Bryn smiled.

Sophie sat up, stretched and said, "You took forever last night. I was starting to get worried but..."

"But what?"

"It's you; I pity the person who fucks with you."

"Ha, ha, now here's the plan for today. A few doors down from the Best Buy is a Staples. I would imagine they have water and snack food there too, but before we go there, I want to go to the used-car lot."

"Cars don't work," Sophie said.

"But old cars do. We've seen them, remember?" Bryn stated.

"You're brilliant!" Matt exclaimed.

"I know. Now get dressed, we have a long day. I need to go see Colin about something," Bryn said and left the apartment.

The warmth of the new sun's rays hit her face and felt good; she paused to take in the moment. Sunny mornings, especially near the coast like she was, weren't so typical. The marine layer from the ocean often hung over the coastal areas till late morning, so seeing the blue sky made her feel hopeful about the day ahead.

No one was moving in the parking lot and the sounds were of nature. She heard birds chirping and the patter of a squirrel in the eucalyptus tree that partially shaded her building. Her respite from it all ended when a familiar voice spoke.

"Good morning, sunshine," Colin said.

"Oh, hey," Bryn said, a bit startled.

"You were having a moment there, I see."

"Yeah, you caught me," Bryn said. A small smile creased her face. She walked over to Colin, who was perched in a small folding chair.

"It's good to remember the beauty in the world."

"Um, I wanted to talk to you."

"Go ahead."

"Do you mind watching over my place? I don't trust those guys, much less others here that might be tempted to pay us a visit. Our stockpiling hasn't been secret."

"You don't have to ask. I'm always watching over everything. I got you covered. So where you off to today?"

Bryn was about to tell him then hesitated. She knew she could trust him, but an odd paranoia came over her. She looked at him, his eyes watching and waiting for the answer.

"To another store."

"You might want to start looking for a car."

Her eyes widened and she felt a bit flush. It was as if

he was reading her mind. "I was thinking the same thing. Maybe stop by a used-car lot."

"Not a bad idea."

"Thanks for all the help."

"My pleasure."

Bryn walked back to her apartment, but her mind raced. She wondered what Colin's story was. She realized she wasn't seeing the world fully; her focus and attention were only on herself and her needs. Last night, she had asked a couple questions, but spent most of her time talking. She wanted to know who this man was, this guardian angel of some sort. How was it he seemed so at ease, so confident? She hadn't seen him leave; he just sat there, like many others in her complex did, but he wasn't like the others at all. Upon her return, she would take time to find out who her new friend was.

"Change of plans, kids. Today we're off to find a car. This walking and pushing carts stuff is over," Bryn said to Matt and Sophie. She was pacing the apartment while the two sat on the couch, staring up at her like children.

"We should have thought about a car day one. Not sure how easy it will be to find one," Matt commented.

"This is exactly why we need to go to Mom's house. She has that old MG," Sophie said then blew a bubble with her gum.

"Enough about Mom's house, we're not going," Bryn snapped.

"I bet that car works," Sophie countered. "You said

old cars, and that thing has to be thirty or forty years old."

"That will probably work," Matt said.

"It won't. It's a two-seat car. We need something bigger," Bryn said.

"You just don't want to go is all. Two seats are better than none," Sophie fired back.

Bryn rolled her eyes and continued with the plan she had thought out. "There are a few used-car lots down off Garnet and Grand."

"This is going to be fun," Matt joked.

"I've got this to help protect us too," Bryn said, holding up her new handgun.

"Whoa, where did you get that? Did the old man give that to you?" Sophie asked. "I want one."

"Let's grab our backpacks. We have a long walk ahead of us," Bryn said, ignoring Sophie's requests to get her own gun.

The three geared up, and under the mid-morning sun they walked out of the complex. Noticeably absent were the three troublemakers. Bryn knew this pleasant absence was the result of the tense incident yesterday and that they wouldn't be gone for long. They might have fled yesterday under threat but would no doubt come back, and at that time it would probably be deadly. Fully aware of how untenable their ability to stay in her apartment was, she hoped they were successful today. Getting a car would give them the mobility to find a safer place to call home.

Sophie constantly kept the pressure on to go to their mother's house, but Bryn wouldn't budge. She wanted nothing to do with her mother. Having lived her entire adult life free of her mother's influences, there was no way she'd give in now.

Matt was perplexed by her resistance and suspected there was something darker, a skeleton residing in Bryn's closet, one she wasn't about to let Matt see just yet.

"This is sort of cool, don't you think?" Matt said with a smile.

"What do you mean?" Bryn asked; sweat glistening on her forehead and face.

"This is like a movie. I feel like I'm on a movie set."

"Only you would think this shit is cool. What a freak," Bryn snapped.

"I think it's cool, Matt, I dig it. Fuck this materialistic capitalist system. It got what was coming to it."

"You're too funny, Soph. Only a princess who was given everything and lived a privileged life with birthday parties that featured ponies, actors and an overabundance of cakes and presents would have such an attitude," Bryn snarled.

"Fuck you, Bryn."

"What happened to you?"

"I grew up. I had nothing to do with that. I wasn't given a choice, but if I have kids, they won't be tortured with such things."

"I would have loved to have been *tortured* as a kid," Matt quipped.

"Don't get me wrong. Mom took care of me; she was misguided."

"She was more than misguided," Bryn snapped.

"I love seeing the duplicity of siblings. Two people raised in the same house, same parents but totally different people. It really shows that it's more about nature versus nurture."

"Don't be quick to assume you know if we were raised the same," Bryn challenged.

"We were, Bryn. Stop being a fucking drama queen."

Bryn grew quiet, electing not to respond. Conversations about her past, specifically her childhood, were off-limits.

Her silence infected the others. Each step they drew closer to their target. People moved about, going through abandoned cars, looking for what they thought was valuable. As if they were invisible, they glided through the maze of cars that littered the street, the odd stranger taking notice for a brief moment then carrying on with whatever they were doing. Occasionally a car would weave through, the rumble of the engine making them stop and look.

With nervous energy Bryn kept touching the grip of the revolver. Having it with her gave her a confidence she hadn't had before. Her life was one absent of such things, and she was a person that was ambivalent on the topic of firearms. She never had a need for one but didn't believe so strongly that they were the source of all evil that she wanted them banned or over-regulated. All she had ever wanted in her life was to be left alone to pursue her dreams unencumbered by others' desires. Never one to engage in political discussions, she avoided those who did as if they had a highly contagious disease.

On the flipside, Sophie had turned into a passionate advocate for every left-leaning cause regardless if it truly affected her.

Bryn looked at this as naïve and vapid, finding those who dwelled on such things needed a job because they clearly had too much time on their hands. Whenever she was cornered on hot topics, she'd just state that the truly huge issues of their society were gone. Poverty in the country wasn't true poverty compared to a villager in central Africa, or that people's rights weren't in jeopardy when looking at those suffering under the strict regimes in North Korea or Cuba. The one issue she found zero connection with was the neo-feminist. The talk of a war on women she found rang hollow. Her opposition to this enraged Sophie, who often labeled her as either blind or dumb. Bryn would counter that by telling her a modern feminist was really a sexist, and that if someone wanted people, all people, to be equal that they should label themselves humanists.

Bryn just didn't have time for all the 'issues' of the modern world and only sought freedom from it all. She believed the only way to get that was to be independent and accept the world was full of good people who sometimes did bad things and bad people who sometimes masked themselves as good. Like the car-riddled street, she viewed life as a maze. If you wanted to succeed, you had to navigate through it. For those who liked to talk, they sat in one place and endlessly discussed the maze without ever taking a step and then would blame their lack of movement or success on others instead of realizing they held themselves back.

"Garnett Street is up ahead, half a block," Matt said.

"Thank God, my feet hurt like hell," Sophie complained.

"If I remember, the first place is called Mike and Son's Auto Sales. Let's keep our fingers crossed," Bryn said.

They reached the corner and stopped to survey the area and car lot. No one was there.

"Looks clear. I can't believe it," Bryn commented after spending a minute eyeing the lot for any movement.

"In fact, the place looks untouched. Are we that lucky?" Matt said.

"Can we please stop talking and go get a damn car?" Sophie moaned.

Bryn again touched the butt of the revolver before taking her first step out into the intersection.

The car lot sat across the street, just one lot off the intersection corner.

They dashed across the street and jumped a small barrier wall that ran the perimeter of the lot and into a row of cars.

Squatting between two cars, they looked at each other nervously.

"Wait. We're being silly," Bryn said and stood up. "Come on, let's go."

Matt and Sophie followed her. Matt's head swiveled in both directions, looking for anyone that might walk up or pose a threat.

Bryn bee lined it for the long trailer that operated as the office. "Matt, find a car you think will work."

"Okay," he replied and started to assess the models and age of cars on the small quarter-acre lot. All the cars were older models, but finding one old enough might be an issue.

The door to the office was locked, no surprise to Bryn. Sitting next to the door was a large rock. Normally this was used to prop the door open; now it would be used to open the door. She picked up the softball-sized rock and began to smash the door handle. It took only a few hits for the cheap handle to break off. She tried to pull the door, but the latch was still holding it closed. "Damn," she cried out.

Movement behind the door startled her; she dropped the rock and pulled the revolver out. Her hands were shaking. "Matt, someone's here."

He immediately stopped what he was doing and raced towards her, his ASP extended and ready.

A click and the door opened.

Bryn stepped back down the worn metal steps and held the pistol at eye level.

"You were always the bull in the china shop," Sophie said, a broad prideful smile on her face.

"How did you get in?" Bryn asked.

"I tried the back door. It was locked, but the lazy bastards left a key exactly where you'd think they'd leave one, under a flower pot," she answered and held the door open.

Matt stopped in his tracks when he saw who it was and laughed out loud. "That's awesome!"

Bryn tucked the revolver back in her waistband and walked in. "Okay, smarty pants, where would the keys be?"

"Um, duh, right where it says KEYS," she replied, pointing to a metal cabinet that hung on the wall.

The offices were nothing more than a thirty-foot rectangular box with windows. Inside there were two rooms, one an office and the other a conference room. A small bathroom divided the two main rooms.

The metal cabinet hung in the office. Bryn walked directly to it and found it locked. She turned to Sophie and said, "Well, any ideas?"

Sophie grabbed a letter opener and a paperweight. She jabbed the letter opener into the tumbler and hammered it with the paperweight until she heard a pop. She turned the letter opener and it worked like a key. "There you go."

"What classes are they teaching you in SF?"

Sophie's only response was to put her index finger to her head and say, "You got the long legs, and I got the curvy butt and brains."

"Whatever, get out of the way," Bryn said and looked at the key chains for anything that would identify what key went to what car. "These guys were organized; I think this is going to go smoother than I thought. C'mon, let's go get ourselves a car," she said, pulling every key out of the cabinet.

Bryn was proud of her sister. In one arm she carried all the keys in a box and the other she wrapped around Sophie in a tight embrace.

They laughed about getting into the office and were lost in making jokes and chatting, and they didn't see who was outside until it was too late.

"Look what we have here," a man said, holding a pistol to Matt's head.

Matt was on his knees and trembling with fear. "I'm sorry, they came up on me. I didn't get a chance to warn you," he cried out.

Bryn and Sophie were frozen in fear on the stairs. A quick look of the lot sorted the situation up for Bryn; they were outnumbered and outgunned. She counted five men and all of them had weapons. Under her breath she whispered to Sophie, "Run back inside, go."

"What do you have in your hand there?" the man said. He pressed the pistol harder into Matt's head. His dark brown hair of unknown length was covered by a ball cap, and the tight fitted T-shirt showcased his muscular build. Overall he looked about five foot ten, but to Bryn he might as well have been a giant. The four other men all looked similar, white, young and ready to do whatever they wanted.

Bryn's insides churned and tightened. She tried to think of a way out of this where Matt was saved, but she couldn't come up with one. Running away was her and Sophie's only option. She hated thinking that Matt would be left to these men and whatever devious things they were capable of, but she couldn't come up with anything.

"Sophie, run," she whispered again.

"Let him go and we'll give you the keys," Sophie cried out.

"It's just that easy, let him go and you'll give us the keys. Maybe we want more than that," the man hollered.

This was exactly what Bryn didn't want to hear. She

knew negotiation with these men was not an option especially when you didn't have leverage.

"You look like a hot piece of ass there," the man said.

"I get the other one," a second man called out, referring to Bryn.

"Listen, guys, we just came here to get a car, but we don't want trouble," Sophie responded.

Bryn's non-responsiveness was making Matt upset, but he had resolved himself to the fact he wouldn't make it out of this. So with this grim prediction he cried out, "Run, girls, run like hell." He lunged from his kneeling position and collided with the man holding him at gunpoint. This forceful impact caused the man to drop the gun. Seeing an opportunity, Matt dove for it, as did the man.

The other men ran towards them, their guns out in front.

Bryn dropped the box of keys, pulled the revolver and headed at them too, in direct contradiction to her own initial thoughts and instincts.

Normally Sophie would have been afraid, but she grabbed the rock and pulled the pepper spray from her pocket. Like her sister, she ran towards the men.

As everyone ran towards an explosive and deadly collision, Matt and the man were locked in a fierce struggle for the loose pistol.

Bryn's heart was pounding hard in her chest, and with the revolver out in front of her, she squeezed off the first round, hitting the second man.

The man fell to the ground hard; he was hit but not dead. He looked at Bryn and raised his pistol, but before he could pull the trigger, she shot him in the face.

Bryn looked for another target, but a volley of fire rained down on her from one of the other men. Two bullets hit her, cutting through her upper right arm and making it impossible for her to hold the revolver. It dropped from her hand and hit the pavement.

The man who had shot her smiled and came towards her, pistol leveled at her head.

The struggle between Matt and the first man ended with Matt losing. A shot rang out from the pile of arms and legs.

Matt groaned and rolled over on his side. His hands were plastered to his stomach.

The man stood up and brushed himself off. He spit on the ground and yelled, "You dumb fat fuck! Now I'm going to kill you!"

Sophie kept running towards them, but her attempt was feeble, and she was tackled to the ground by one of the men. He sat on top of her; a toothy grin told her she would be punished for their resistance.

Bryn, Sophie and Matt tried to fight back, but the odds were not in their favor. They had managed to kill one, but it was just too much.

Bryn tried to stand, but the two men guarding her pushed her back to her knees, their pistols held at her head. Blood poured out of her wounds and pooled on the pavement.

"Get up, motherfucker!" the man yelled at Matt.

Matt didn't answer; he squirmed on the ground in pain in a thick puddle of blood.

The man bent down and grabbed him by the back of his shirt and pulled him up. "Damn, you're a heavy fuck." He rammed his pistol in Matt's mouth and yelled out, "Time to die."

Matt looked up at him. Tears flowed from his eyes as he knew his time on earth was close to an end.

Sophie shrieked with sorrow for Matt. "Please don't kill him, please! I'll do whatever you want, just don't kill him."

"Listen, bitch, we don't have to barter with you. We'll take whatever we want. Now shut up before I bust your pretty mouth open!"

"You're a piece of shit, and when I get up, I'm going to kill you!" Bryn yelled.

"Ha, ha, do you hear this bitch?" The man laughed. "She's going to kill me, ha!"

Bryn stared at him hard; the pain in her arm had gone as the rage acted as a painkiller. "That's right; I'm going to kill you."

"We shall see," the man said. He put his full attention back on Matt and began to squeeze the trigger.

A rifle shot cracked.

One of the men watching over Bryn dropped to the ground dead. The back of his head was missing.

The man holding the pistol on Matt looked around and yelled, "Who the fuck is that?"

A second shot cracked, hitting the second man next to Bryn. Again that shot was true, hitting him in the head. He fell backwards, landing hard on the ground.

Now only two men remained, the first man standing

over Matt and the man with Sophie.

Bryn took advantage of the situation and grabbed a pistol from one of her dead attackers. She turned and shot the man next to Sophie several times.

Only the first man remained. He screamed out, "Where the fuck are you?" He slowly began to back away, the pistol he held in his tight grasp out in front of him. Out of fear he began to pull the trigger repeatedly until the pistol clicked with the slide locked back; he was empty. He pivoted, but Bryn was standing in his way.

"I told you I was going to kill you," she said and pulled the trigger.

Vista, CA

The slight breeze felt good on Vincent's face. The noise of the wood blinds banging against the windowsill had awakened him. The sound brought back memories of Idaho and the cool breezes that would whip through his parent's house just before a summer thunderstorm. He missed home but one incident after another pushed his dream of seeing it again further away.

His vision was still blurry, so he blinked repeatedly in an attempt to focus. He assumed he had probably hit his head hard. He gazed around the quaintly decorated room. Trinkets adorned the small shelves and tops of all the furniture. In the air was a faint smell of lavender. He began to wonder if he had awoken in his grandmother's house in

Challis, Idaho. When he adjusted himself in the bed, a sharp pain emanated from his right foot. He tossed off the sheets and looked at a tight bandage. He ran his hands across the textured fabric until he found the center of the pain. Exhaling deeply, he tried to recall how he had arrived where he was. He remembered the helicopter crash but not much after. He glanced around the room, looking for his clothes, but saw nothing. The shorts he had on were not his, and by the way his wound had been treated and the condition of the room, he assumed those who had rescued him were good people.

The door opening startled him. He adjusted himself, preparing to meet whoever had rescued him. The door had slowly creaked open not more than nine inches when a child's head appeared from around it. The boy saw Vincent awake and staring at him. Shyly, he tucked his head back. He could hear unintelligible whispering followed by a man's voice.

"Close that door and leave him alone!"

The children listened to the unseen man and scurried away without closing the door.

Vincent sat farther up in the bed and said, "Hello?"

The door opened fully to reveal the man; he didn't recognize his face, but he must be in safe hands otherwise why the care. The man was young, probably similar in age to him.

He stepped into the room and said, "How are you feeling?"

"I'm still above ground. That's always good," he replied.

"Are you hungry?" he asked.

"I am."

"Good, I'll go get some food," he said, then turned around.

"Wait. Don't go just yet. I have questions, a lot of questions."

"Let's answer your questions after you eat."

"I guess I can wait a bit longer."

Before he left, he approached the bed, put out his hand, and said, "I'm Steven."

Vincent took his hand and shook it. "I'm—"

"Sergeant Gunner Vincent, United States Marine Corps. I know," he answered confidently.

He looked oddly at him, not knowing how he knew his name.

Pointing at his chest, he said, "Your dog tags and you had your identification in your wallet. We didn't mean to be nosy; my father just wanted to see who you were."

"Of course, I'd do the same thing. Where am I?"

"Unless you need something else besides your questions answered, I'll go get your food."

As he stepped toward the door, Vincent asked, "Can you answer me this, where am I?"

"You're at my father's house."

"It looks like a farm," he said, looking out the window.

"It is."

"What do you grow?"

"Sergeant, I told you that your questions will be answered, but later. Please, you've been hurt badly. You need your rest so you can heal."

"Fine, I'll stop, but you must understand that I'm curious. I somehow live after that and get rescued. If my body didn't hurt so bad, I'd swear I was in heaven."

"You're not in heaven; I can guarantee that. With everything that has happened, I'd say we might be in hell. Now lie back and rest. I'll be back soon with lunch," he said and left, closing the door behind her.

He adjusted in the bed in hopes it would alleviate the pain, but it didn't. His surviving being thrown from the helicopter was nothing short of a miracle. He didn't know the reason, but he was meant to live. He was sure the *Harpers Ferry* had sent another helicopter to search for them. The pain spiked in his foot and felt like an electric shock. He scrunched his face in pain and decided he needed to heed her advice. If he was going to get word back to the ship, he needed to be healthy. He sank into the thick pillows and closed his eyes.

San Diego, CA

Bryn stood over the man. Thick red blood oozed from the bullet hole in his face. She aimed the pistol and pulled the trigger again. It wasn't necessary, as he was dead; she did it solely for her own satisfaction.

Unsure of who fired the rifle shots, she looked across

the street and saw a man waving and with his other hand he held up the rifle.

She waved back. After what had happened, she was skeptical, but what could she do? She thought. If they wanted her, Sophie or Matt dead, they easily could have done it. She had to assume this person was decent and was saving them.

Matt moaned.

Both she and Sophie ran to him.

"We're going to get you help," Bryn said.

Matt's wound was serious. He had taken a point-blank gunshot to the stomach and he was bleeding badly. The pain was immense; he cried and kept begging for them to do something.

"What are we going to do?" Sophie asked.

"We're going to help him. Now is not the time to be having this discussion. I'm going to see if one of these cars will work," Bryn said and ran to the box lying where she had dropped it.

The hard patter of feet caught her attention and she spun around. The pistol still in her hand, she held it out. The trembling she had experienced the first time she handled a gun was gone. "Stop right there. Don't even think about doing anything."

"Whoa, don't shoot. We were the ones that saved you," the man said, frozen to the spot fifteen feet from Sophie and Matt.

"I need to help my friend."

"I'm a doctor and I can help your friend," the man said.

She started to walk back towards him when she saw three other men running in their direction. "Don't fuck with me, us! I'll kill you like I killed that other fuck!"

The other men caught up to the first and stopped. "Let's be clear I killed three of them."

"Who are you?" Bryn asked.

"We're the good guys. I'm Nicholas McNeil, and we're here to help."

Once an understanding was established, Brent and Alex went to work trying to find cars that worked.

Bryn's right arm was injured, but that didn't stop her trying to also go to work.

Nicholas stopped her. "Hey, your arm needs to be bandaged up. It looks like you took a couple hits. Doesn't that hurt?"

She looked down at her bloody and swollen arm. It throbbed, but her adrenaline was still high. Putting on a tougher persona, she shrugged it off. "It's a flesh wound. I'll be fine."

"No, it won't. You're not doing yourself any favors by sucking up the pain," Nicholas reminded her as he grabbed some items from his trauma kit. He ripped open a pad and began to clean the wound.

She pouted as she watched Alex and Brent begin their search. In the rear of the lot she saw a red Bronco and called out, "The red Bronco is mine. I'm calling that!"

Brent and Alex looked back. Alex waved and headed for it.

"Looks like we weren't the only ones with this idea," Nicholas said.

"Yeah, kind of a no-brainer, just happens that everyone showed up on the same day," Bryn responded as she watched him apply antibiotic ointment.

"Lucky for you the rounds went clean through. Totally missed the bone."

"Can you hurry up?" she asked, her patience almost tapped as she watched Brent and Alex walk up to the Bronco and peer into the windows.

"Calm down. You claimed it, it's yours."

She cocked her head and asked, "No one is that nice."

"Well, I am, or at least I'd like to think I am. I don't know what's happening or how this shit is all going to work itself out, but I can't sit back and allow what I saw happen when I can do something about it."

"You are a nice guy, wow," she said.

"Don't mistake kindness for weakness. My family and friends come first, and if you are in my way or are hurting others for no reason, I'll unleash my wrath on you."

"A nice guy that kills, I like it," she said a bit flirtatiously.

"I try to do the right thing to a point."

"Hey, don't smash the window!" she hollered out to Alex and Brent.

Brent was about to swing a large stick at the driver's window.

"I have the key here and that's my car."

Brent gave her a hard look.

"Your friend there isn't so nice, though," she said.

"He's not nice and he's not my friend," Nicolas responded. He gently patted her arm and continued, "All done. Let's go see if your new car runs."

Bryn pushed past Brent, unlocked the Bronco and climbed in. She paused and said a quick prayer before turning the key. The Bronco roared to life. Its V-8 engine grumbled and spit as she pressed the accelerator. "Yes!"

Brent was in earshot and shouted out, "We should get it!"

"We were here first," Bryn countered.

"Yeah, but if we didn't help, you'd be dead and we'd just take it anyway."

Bryn scrunched her face. She couldn't argue with that logic.

"Nic, we need to get him out of here. I did all I can do here; I need to take him to my clinic," Proctor called out. He had bandaged and stopped the bleeding with the trauma kit Nicholas had brought, but the bullet was still inside. "I need to operate on him."

"Put him in the back of my truck!" Bryn hollered.

Nicholas gave her a glance but let it go. He appreciated her spunkiness, and the timing wasn't right to argue about a car. A man's life hung in the balance.

Brent stepped up to the driver's window, looked at Bryn and declared, "Don't think you'll keep this."

Bryn winked at him and drove over to Matt.

"We need another car!" Brent screamed.

"And we'll get one. We're splitting up. Proctor, do you feel safe enough to take him back to your office?"

"Yeah, I feel safe enough, but I need some help," he

answered. Proctor wiped the blood from his hands on his jeans.

Nicholas really liked Proctor; he was a no-nonsense man, smart, witty and tough. He had a lean build and dark hair he kept cut short, but liked to keep a few days of stubble on his face at all times. "Take the girl with you and Brent."

"I'm staying here to help find another car since you gave that one to them," Brent sulked.

"We'll find another car or more. Just go," Nicholas ordered.

Brent gave him a sour look and walked over to Proctor.

"Take his legs and help me put him in the back," Proctor said to Brent.

They loaded Matt up and soon left for Proctor's clinic in Poway, fifteen miles away.

Nicholas watched them drive off. His practical mind stepped in and put forward the idea that what he was doing wasn't smart. He rebuffed this and told himself that if he and his family were to survive, they'd need alliances and others. Maybe these new people would be a part or just people they'd meet along the way. Anyway, he hoped karma existed, because he knew one day he'd need to be rescued too.

Calexico, CA

Michael was tired and his body ached. The drive through

the night had been taxing, but he declared that he wouldn't sleep until he crossed into the United States. Curiosity ran strong in him, so he took the risk and drove to the border checkpoints east of Mexicali. He wanted to see if anyone was there or if they had pulled back since the attacks. What he found surprised him; the border was wide open. The stations usually manned by border patrol agents were vacant. He drove across as easy as an illegal crossing the Rio Grande. This told him the attacks had done enough damage that critical parts of government had fragmented and abandoned their posts. He didn't know if the border was left open because of an order or because the individual agents couldn't get there or just decided not to show up.

The EMP certainly had created havoc, but coupled with nuclear strikes against major cities, the entire country was paralyzed. His knowledge of how the government worked told him that all essential personnel were bunkered down across the country; hundreds of feet down they were living in a luxury that many Americans had known. These lucky few who happened to find themselves protected would not know the horrors that would soon visit most of the population. Where this war was going was unknown, but what he did know was that the country he had worked for and pledged his life to for over twenty years was gone.

He didn't know his role in the EMP strike but could only assume he had been sent to stop it. Why he was on that ship was the nagging question. The stress of the past three days and the injuries he had suffered had taken a lot out of him. He found this stress had impacted his memory. He needed rest and soon.

With the desert flat and expansive all around him, he headed north.

"Where's a good spot to catch a few hours of sleep?" he muttered out loud.

To the west he spotted a gravel pit; this seemed like a good place to hide out. Who would be needing gravel in a post-EMP world? He asked himself.

He took the next left and drove a mile when the gas light came on. Oddly a smile cracked his rugged face. He considered himself lucky that he had made it this far without having to refuel.

Seeing Jose again was something that would never happen, but he owed his life to that man and his family. He didn't know what bad things he had done, but Michael knew he wasn't a bad man, just a man trying to make his way in the world. So often he had met people, many good that made bad decisions. For the most part that's how he viewed most people. This didn't mean he would have to show mercy to those people if his life was in jeopardy. If a good person decided one day to do a bad thing and it put him in the crosshairs, he'd have no remorse in killing them. It wasn't personal to him; it just was what it was.

His eyes grew heavy and he dozed off. The car veered off the dirt road and into a drainage ditch. He woke up and jerked the car hard back onto the road and saved himself from crashing. He looked ahead through the grimy windshield and saw the gravel pit was only a mile away.

"Stay awake," he said, loudly smacking himself.

He finished the drive and pulled into the facility slowly, keeping an eye out for who or what might be there that could be a threat. Situational awareness came naturally to him. A slow drive around gave him the confidence that it was vacant. He pulled behind a small mountain of rock and dirt and parked. He stepped out and again scanned the area. He was beyond tired, but one mistake in this world meant death, and he wasn't so tired that he wanted the eternal sleep.

A small utility shed was fifty feet away. He made for that and found it unlocked. Inside he found tools and other small items.

"Jackpot," he said when he found a stack of tarps. He positioned them into a small bed, but before he curled up, he secured the door. "This is going to feel good," he said as he lay down. Just as he drifted off to sleep, another name came to him. He opened his eyes and blurted out, "Viktor Azamov."

Vista, CA

Vincent wiped his mouth with the paper towel napkin and melted into the pillows content. "That was one of the best lunches I've ever had, God how I've missed home cooked meal.

"It was freeze-dried," Steve laughed.

"Freeze-dried?"

"Yes, now if you're up to it, my father wants to talk with you."

"Uh, sure."

"Good, I'll be right back," Steven said and left.

Steve left the door open, giving Vincent the ability to hear murmurs down the hall. He couldn't quite make out what the people were saying, but it didn't make much difference, as within moments of her departure, a man stepped into the room. He was tall, white-haired, clean-shaven and handsome. If Vincent was to guess, he'd say he was in his mid-sixties. The man walked to the chair that sat next to the window. He grabbed it and positioned it closer to the side of the bed. Vincent just stared nervously at him. After the man sat down, he smoothed out his trousers and crossed his legs. Placing his hands on his knee, he cleared his throat and looked at Vincent.

"Hello, sir," Vincent greeted the man.

"I want to thank you for rescuing me from the chopper and taking—"

"No need to thank us," the man interrupted.

"Okay," Vincent said and then shut up. He didn't know what to say. The man made him feel apprehensive.

"Sergeant, I have some questions for you, so I'll just

Vincent paused for a moment. He looked at the man sitting next to him. He seemed familiar, but he knew he'd never met him before. He was dressed in jeans and a buttoned-up collared shirt. His clothes were clean, but his jeans showed the stains of work. Vincent studied his hands and saw that they too showed the marks of labor. His knuckles looked rough, and some fresh scratches were visible. "I'm from a Marine Expeditionary Unit. We were coming back from deployment when the war started. Our ships are headed to Camp Pendleton, but I was on a mission to rescue an officer's family and take them to safety."

"War?"

"Yes, we are at war with Russia. It appears they struck first with an EMP, we retaliated, and they struck back with nuclear weapons."

The man raised his eyebrows. This was the first he had heard of such a thing. "There's been a nuclear war?"

"Yes, sir."

"What do you know?"

"I know what I know, sir, nothing more," Vincent answered.

"That's truth there," the man said.

"You know me. Who are you?" Vincent asked.

"My name is Roger Puller."

"Wait a minute, Roger Puller, like Roger Puller the billionaire? You're the guy who developed smart weapons."

"There's nothing smart about a weapon," Roger said and looked down.

"No, that stuff is cool. Those 40mm grenades with the self-propulsion and guidance, they're amazing."

"Enough, you don't know everything about me. I created those systems decades ago, only seven years ago did they go into use. I have since regretted all the things I did. Since you've heard of me, you'll know that I sold Puller Defense Industries and have put myself as far away from my past as I could."

"I did see something on the news; you've become quite the peace advocate."

Roger exhaled heavily and looked at Vincent. His eyes had a look like they were weighted down by years of regret and sorrow. "That was the old me. I'm a new man now with a new mission in life."

"I apologize; I didn't mean to bring up things that are sensitive. By the way, thank you for rescuing me and taking me in."

"That's what we do."

"I have to ask, how old are you? You're like in your sixties now, and I saw two young kids out there."

"They are my blessings; they're adopted. Steve is my only biological child."

"Sorry, I'm prying."

"Pay no mind. So you're holding up."

"Yeah, I guess. I need to contact my ship, though, and inform them I'm alive."

"In good time, you need to rest more. Give it a day," Roger said and patted his leg.

Vincent thought it odd he wasn't asking more questions or that he didn't seem freaked out about the news that the country was at war.

"I really need to contact them."

"Well, Sergeant Vincent. You broke your foot badly. You're not going anywhere anytime soon," the man said, pointing at his bandaged foot. "Your fellow Marines will be at Camp Pendleton. They're not going anywhere. Look at this as R&R."

He didn't like not being able to reach out, but he'd be patient a bit longer. Soon he'd have to stress the importance. However, he couldn't shrug off the odd feeling he had about Roger. He wasn't concerned and he seemed too calm.

"I'll let you rest. Steve will bring you dinner later."

"Thanks again."

Roger left and closed the door.

Vincent looked out the window. The sun was high in the blue sky. He marveled that the world didn't take notice of the troubles happening. The sun rose and set and life went on. Soon thoughts crept to his parents and then to his situation. Maybe the crash and his surviving it was meant to happen. He was sure they thought him dead along with the others. If he ever had a reason not to go back, this was it, but soon that thought was squashed by his devotion to the Marines. Leaving under these circumstances seemed wrong and dishonest, it challenged his integrity. He didn't want to think about it anymore, so he shook his head in an attempt to clear his thoughts. Rest was critical, he needed it, and his foot needed to heal. He was no good to himself or his fellow Marines with a broken foot. Today he'd rest; tomorrow, well, he'd make that decision then.

San Diego, CA

The search for another car proved disappointing. The Bronco was the only operational vehicle there. They visited another lot down the street, but that too proved futile. Unable to find one and the day's light sinking into the horizon, Nicholas questioned his allowing Bryn to claim the

Bronco. He could hear Becky now questioning his kindness, especially to a young attractive woman. Maybe his kindness this time had been weakness. The other problem he had was Frank was expecting the Dodge back. He came to the determination that he'd have to let him down or enlist Bryn to help him.

"It's getting dark, and I don't want to be on the roads at night," Nicholas said.

"I need to go get my sister and friend," Bryn said.

Alex looked over and optimistically said, "Don't fret, Nic, there's always tomorrow."

"Well, I have to give the Dodge back to my father-in-law."

Bryn couldn't help but feel for his plight and had also come to a realization that she needed more friends in order to survive. She prided herself on being a quick judge of character, and Nicholas and Alex seemed like good people. They had to be; they'd had every opportunity to hurt her but hadn't. What was holding them back was their own deep and true goodness.

"You can use my Bronco to find another car. I owe you that," she offered.

Nicholas looked at her and said, "You'd do that?"

"How can I not offer? You saved our lives and your friend is caring for Matt."

"You don't know me, but I'm never one for charity, but this circumstance is unique. I'll take you up on that."

"I love when people can work together," Alex said, a big grin on his face.

"And you, I like you," Bryn said.

"Is it my boyish good looks or that I'm just an all-around good guy?" Alex joked.

During the entire day's journey, Alex had been charming, resourceful and had kept an even-keel attitude that she found refreshing. She wasn't attracted to him, but she could see them being friends. She guessed he was twenty years her senior or a little less, so it was more of a big-brother attraction. Nicholas too was the same age spread as Alex, but she did feel a slight pull. It was clear and he established he was married, but ever since she was a young woman, she liked older men. Nicholas was handsome, confident and strong but had compassion, a trait that she found made a person human and one she always looked for in a man.

"I guess this makes us partners for now," Nicholas said.

"Partners it is."

"Let's work out logistics, then," Nicholas said, getting right to business.

As they drove the car-riddled highway towards Proctor's clinic, they worked out how they'd work together. Nicholas wanted to ensure he'd have access to her car, and in order to guarantee that, he wanted them close by. After a bit of discussion the plan was set. Bryn and Sophie would stay with him while Matt would stay at Proctor's house under his care.

Nicholas told Bryn where he lived and that he was semi-prepared with equipment, food and water.

She had known that morning her time was coming to an end at Sycamore Grove, and this plan gave her a way

THE DEFIANT: GRID DOWN

out. It was a hasty decision, but she didn't feel there was a lot of time to sit and ponder. How she would work out a permanent thing with Nicholas wasn't clear to her, but she'd find a way, she just needed to get out of her place.

They reached Proctor's clinic, but the good news of plans and partnerships vaporized the moment they walked in the house.

"I did everything I could, but he had lost too much blood," Proctor said. His face showed the anguish that all were feeling. Matt was a stranger to him, but Proctor was a sensitive man. He felt Sophie's pain and wished he could have done something, but it was beyond his abilities and resources.

Sophie was in the examination room with Matt's body, wailing.

Bryn ran to her.

"Sorry," Nicholas said to Proctor.

"I'm sorry I couldn't fix him."

"What do you recommend we do with the body?" Nicholas asked.

"Just toss it in the dumpster," Brent said.

"Are you always an asshole, or is today just asshole day for Brent?" Proctor asked. It had only taken Proctor a couple hours to see Brent for what he was, an annoying prick.

"That's not going to happen. We will bury him. Let's get him wrapped up in something, and we'll take his body wherever the girls want to take him."

Bryn walked in and, after overhearing their conversation, said, "Thank you Nic, let's take him with us. I'll be honest I didn't know him all that long, but in the short time we did spend together, I found him to be a great guy. I want to honor that by giving him what he deserves, a proper burial."

"And we'll do that, but I don't want to be a pest about timing. We need to go. I really don't want to be on the roads at night, and I need to drop off the Dodge."

"We're getting rid of the car without having another?" Brent barked.

"Brent, it's taken care of. Bryn's going to allow us to use hers until we can find cars for all of us," Alex said.

"This is such bullshit. That truck should be ours."

Bryn raised her middle finger at Brent.

"Fuck you!" Brent fired back at her.

"Shut up, Brent, and go help carry Matt's body out to the Bronco," Nicholas ordered.

"I'm done helping. This entire day has been a failure. There were two things I needed, a car and that prescription."

Brent had a point; the day was partially a failure. They hadn't found more vehicles and not one item was collected from the list.

"Do you have any suggestions, besides bitching?" Alex asked.

"Yes, we keep the Bronco."

"That's not going to happen," Nicholas said.

"C'mon, Brent, you can't just complain. If you have something to add, please do; otherwise do what Nic said and shut up," Alex said.

"Fuck you."

Alex took a step towards Brent, who was so enraged he didn't back away.

"Look at you acting like a bully cop," Brent scolded.

"You are not winning any friends," Alex said.

Brent huffed and stormed off. A moment later they heard the front door open and close.

"What a piece of work," Alex said, shaking his head in astonishment at Brent's behavior.

"You've seen nothing. That's him being nice," Nicholas joked.

Wrapping Matt in several white sheets, they slowly carried him from the examination room through the darkening clinic.

"I can't find the keys. Where are the keys?" Bryn asked. She was crawling on her hands and knees, looking on the floor.

"The fucking Bronco is gone!" Alex cried out.

"Brent took the Bronco, that motherfucker!" Nicholas yelled.

"What do we do?" Proctor asked, referencing Matt's body.

"Put him in the trunk. I'll have to drop off the Dodge later."

"Where do you think he went?" Bryn asked.

"It doesn't matter. He has to come home sometime, and when he does, we'll be there waiting for him," Nicolas said.

Carlsbad, CA

After dropping Proctor at home, he drove as fast as the car-riddled highway would allow him. He hated that he had to drive at night; it was like driving blind with no ability to spot an ambush or see danger. His luck held and he arrived safely, but that luck was about to run out.

When Nicholas walked into the house, Becky cried out, "You're safe, thank God." She wrapped her arms around him and kissed his cheek. After her embrace she looked up and saw the others. "We have guests?"

"Becky, this is Bryn and Sophie. We saved them earlier today. It's a long story."

"Hi, I'm Alex."

"You look familiar," Becky said, referring to Alex.

"Where's Abigail?" Nicholas asked.

"In her room. Are you okay? Brent mentioned you were in a fight today."

"You've seen Brent?"

"I saw him and Chandler not an hour ago. They stopped by and said you were running late and that there had been some trouble."

"No, things aren't fine. I need to go visit our mutual friend and neighbor Brent."

"What's going on?" Becky asked, concerned.

"More trouble is coming, but this time to that asshole," Nicholas said. His temper flared, and he was ready for a fight once and for all.

He marched out of the house and into the darkness of the night.

Bryn, Sophie and Alex followed him out.

Nicholas could hear Brent talking with what sounded like a few people.

When he began walking down his driveway, Brent called out, "Who is that?"

"It's Nicholas."

"You're not welcome on my property. Leave now!" Brent ordered and put a large beam from his flashlight on him.

Undeterred, Nicholas walked right up to Brent and punched him squarely in the face.

Brent reeled back, lost his balance and fell hard to the ground.

"Hold on. Stop," Chandler barked, stepping in front of Nicholas.

"Get out of my way, Chandler. This is between this asshole and me."

"No, no, it isn't. What Brent did was for the community. He told me you found this truck and gave it away."

"It's not like that."

"You can't give away what's not yours," Bryn interjected.

"I don't know who you are, but this doesn't concern you either."

"Oh yes it does. He stole my truck."

"Chandler, you weren't there today. You don't know what's going on," Nicholas charged.

"You're right, I wasn't, but is Brent lying?"

The headlights of the Bronco were on, providing enough light for everyone to see each other.

Brent scurried off the ground and stood. Blood ran from his nose down his face and across his lips. "Fuck you, Nicholas; you're not getting this truck. This is the community's now, not mine."

"It's more than the truck, Brent, and you know it. You took it, leaving us to scramble and get home. You abandoned us."

Brent stepped towards Nicholas, but out of nowhere Bryn stepped forward and hit him with a punch to the side of the face.

"Stop it now!" Chandler screamed.

Brent was shocked by the hit and in his anger lost control and pulled the pistol Nicholas had given him earlier. "Get off my property, now!" he screamed, pointing the pistol at Nicholas.

Bryn reacted by pulling hers and pointing it at Brent.

"Everyone, stop. Put the guns down!" Chandler screamed.

Nicholas raised his hands, showing he was holding a gun and said, "Are you going to shoot me, Brent? Is that what you're going to do?"

"I should. You came on my property, hit me, and then your new girlfriend hit me. That's assault, and I'm within my right to defend myself!"

"Just know that if you pull that trigger, that'll be your death sentence. I'll shoot you and take my truck back," Bryn warned him.

Chandler still stood in between everyone, his arms raised as he attempted to get the situation under control.

Alex had taken a step to the right and was assessing how he could also diffuse the volatile scene.

Sophie was holding back. She too had stepped to the side and was ready to pounce on Brent.

"Give Bryn back the truck. She's offered to allow us to use it as long as we need. She and her sister will be staying with me until we find another."

"No," Brent snapped.

"As the elected leader of this community, here is what I propose. The truck belongs to Bryn, but since she's willing to let us use it, we'll keep it parked here. We will give it back to you once we have found other cars. This is my compromise," Chandler said.

Nicholas thought about it, and it seemed fair. He looked to Bryn, who still held the pistol out. "It's reasonable."

"I want to shoot. Can I please shoot him?" Bryn said.

"Bryn, don't do it. They saved us today. It's a decent deal."

She lowered the pistol.

Brent followed suit and lowered his.

"Give me my pistol back now," Nicholas ordered Brent.

Brent hesitated.

"Give Nic back his gun," Chandler demanded.

"Here," Brent said, holding it out.

Nicholas snatched it and tucked it in his waistband.

"Now can everyone go back to their respective homes? We'll start again tomorrow looking for a car, okay?" Chandler said.

Nicholas, Bryn and Sophie disengaged and walked back to his home.

Watching them walk into the night, Brent grinned. He felt like he won more out of this feud. He caressed the Bronco keys with his thumb and with a chuckle pocketed them.

CHAPTER 4

"It is in your moments of decision that your destiny is forged." – Anonymous

Carlsbad, CA

Nicholas found it impossible to sleep. The events of yesterday kept replaying in his mind. Had he done the right thing? He thought he had. Becky didn't openly challenge him, but she asked him several questions that led him to believe she thought he might have miscalculated. She also made mention of her parents. This was a topic he was aware of, but he put it in the back of his mind. Frank had made his decision not to come there, and for now he needed the car. It was also prominent in his mind that leaving them alone was dangerous, so he'd have to find time to check on them today.

Sick of tossing and turning, he got out of bed. He thought a stroll through his house might make him feel better.

"Where are you going?" Becky asked.

"Oh, hi, I hope I didn't wake you," he replied.

"I haven't been able to sleep. I'm assuming you're the same way."

"Yes."

"Honey, I've been thinking. I want to leave right away, tomorrow if possible. After what I saw and that horrible fight you experienced, I don't want to stay here anymore."

These words were music to his ears, but just how was he going to leave without a vehicle. "I agree, but we still need a car."

"So I was thinking. How about asking those girls to come?"

"Really?"

"Yeah."

"Hold on," he said and flicked the switch on the lantern to low. "I want to see your face, make sure you're not making a face."

"I'm serious. I'm scared, and I just want to go somewhere there are not many people. So that got me thinking too. I think we should head to Montana instead of Palm Desert."

"You want to go to Uncle Jim's ranch? That's a hell of a drive."

"His place is huge, and he has like two hundred acres. I think we can be safe there."

Nicholas sat in silence, thinking about what she had just proposed. He wasn't against the idea; it just had some parts that he couldn't guarantee would work.

"What about your parents?"

"I can't worry about them. I think we should drop the car off first, of course, tell them where we're going, give him a map even, and let it go at that. I can't risk Abigail by staying in the city."

"Okay, let me talk to Bryn and Sophie in the morning," he said and began to head to the door.

"Where ya going?" she asked.

"I still want to pace around and think."

She tossed back the sheets and said, "I've got something else that will make you forget about the crappy day you had yesterday."

"Hmm, serious?"

"Absolutely, get back in bed now," she purred.

Not asking a second time, he jumped back in bed.

Yesterday was a glimpse of what would soon be a widespread problem, and the longer they stayed, scavengers would end up in his neighborhood looking for what they could find. It was only a matter of when not if.

After his confrontation with Brent, he had also lost any desire to work with Chandler or any of his neighbors, so when Becky brought forward her thoughts, Nicholas embraced it. He just needed to see how far his partnership went with Bryn and Sophie, so he sat them down the moment the sun rose and presented it.

"I know we just met not twenty-four hours ago, but I can see you're a good guy, nice family and you have things we'll need. I would say I'm surprised you're asking me, though; I don't offer anything but a vehicle, and I only have it because you're letting me have it. I think this deal is better for me than you," Bryn said.

"I don't know, Bryn, we still need to see how Mom's doing," Sophie added.

"We don't have time to check on Mom."

"Wait. You have a parent close by? Of course we need to check on them. Why wouldn't you?" Nicholas commented.

"Nic, there's too much to go into with this topic."

"Every time I bring Mom up, you freak out, you say this or that. What the hell is wrong with you?" Sophie said, slamming her fist down.

Bryn sat and stewed on what Sophie just said.

"Nic, thanks, but we'll be checking on her before we leave."

"Fine, let's add her address…"

"She let Edward touch me," Bryn said just above a whisper.

"What?" Sophie asked.

Nicholas thought he heard but kept quiet.

Becky was also in the room with Abigail. "Come on, Abby."

"Mom, I want to stay and be a part of this conversation. I have a say, and Dad hasn't checked on my friends."

"Be quiet, everyone," Nicholas said.

Sophie moved closer to Bryn and touched her hand. "Did I hear you correctly?"

"Mom knew he was coming into my room. I told her, but she did nothing. I threatened to tell someone else, but he turned the tables on me. I caught him going into your room; you were so young, so little. I stopped him. He told me the only way to prevent him from hurting you was if I kept quiet and allowed him to do what he wanted to me," Bryn said, her voice cracking as she spoke. Tears welled up in her eyes.

"Oh, Bryn, I never knew. I swear, had I known..."
Sophie said and began to tear up too.

"I'll just step out," Nicholas said and stood.

"No, stay. I want everyone here to know. I've kept this a secret too long, and if we're partners in whatever we're doing, you need to know me."

Nicholas was blown away by what she just said. Her ability to expose something so private and raw hit home for him. He sat back down on the love seat and let her continue.

Sophie cradled Bryn and held her tightly. "Oh, sweetie, I never knew. I'm so sorry."

Bryn openly cried and held Sophie.

Nicholas watched in amazement this display of love and sisterhood. He looked over at Becky and nodded.

Becky and Abigail were also crying now.

The tears became contagious as a few tears streamed down Nicholas' face.

He didn't know how much time had gone by, but it felt like an eternity. However, he couldn't stop this moment; this was something special. It needed to end when Bryn wanted it to.

Wiping the tears away, Bryn sat up and said, "Now you know why I hate Mom and why I don't want anything to do with her."

"I hate her too. I can't believe she allowed that to happen to you. I'm so sorry."

"Is it safe to say checking on your mother is off the list?" Nicholas joked in an attempt to lighten the mood.

"Off the list," Bryn confirmed.

Vista, CA

A knock on the door make him jump. He was rehearsing what to say so he could convince Steve to let him go make a call.

Steve peered around the corner and asked, "Good time?"

"Absolutely, come on in. I'm so hungry I could eat a bear," Vincent replied hopping over to the bed with glee.

He quickly walked in, placed the tray next to him, "We don't have bear so I hope eggs and bacon will do."

"Are you kidding me, I bet they'll be the best eggs and bacon I've ever had. You guys are feeding me like royalty," he said staring at the food, his mouth watering.

"Enjoy your breakfast. I'll come back shortly to get the tray. We have a lot to do to get ready," Steve said and went for the door.

"I need to contact my ship or my unit, something."

"I'll let my father know, but I have things to do."

The door closed but within minutes opened again. Vincent expected to see Steve but it was a little boy who popped his head in.

The boy saw him and nervously pulled it back again.

"Hey, no, come on in, I'd like to have company," Vincent said.

The boy sheepishly stepped further into the room, his hands stuffed in his pocket.

"What's your name?"

"Are you coming with us?"

"What?"

"Are you coming with us?"

"Uhh . . . no," Vincent said.

"Where are you from?"

"Aren't you full of questions?"

The boy walked over and sat down next to him. "My brother said you survived a helicopter crash. Was it scary?"

"You're very inquisitive. I think it's my turn to ask a couple questions."

"Sure," the boy said with a broad smile.

"What city are we in?"

"Vista."

"Where are you from?"

"I'm originally from Idaho," Vincent looked at the boy. He thought about how well mannered and mature he seemed for his age. He guessed that he was about eight years old. His sandy blond hair was cut short, and his clothes showed a boy who seemed sheltered, a solid-colored blue polo-type shirt, jeans, and white socks. Vincent smiled and continued. "When are you leaving?"

"My father wants to leave tomorrow."

"How many in your family?"

"Just dad, Steve, me and my sister."

"Sorry about your mom."

"Me too. Say, you ever kill anyone?"

Now Vincent looked shocked. "How old are you?"

"Answer the question."

Steve suddenly appeared and barked at the boy. "Away with you. Go see dad in the garage."

The boy immediately walked out.

"Nice boy" Vincent said.

"Sometimes," Steve replied.

"So, were you eavesdropping on us?"

"No, I heard voices up here, so I came to see what was going on."

"So you're leaving tomorrow?"

"Yes, it's not secret now, thank you Zach."

"So that's his name? Hmm, he looks like a Zach."

"What were you planning on doing with me?"

"Since the cat's out of the bag, I'll tell you. My father was just going to give you the keys to the house; it's yours. We won't need it anymore."

"Huh, you were going to give me the house?"

"Not give you, but we're abandoning it. If you want it, it's yours."

Vincent didn't know how to process this. Everything had happened so quickly. Just three days ago he was excited to come home from a long combat deployment; then his world ended. Even for a man who had been through much, this was a lot to tackle.

"If you'll excuse me, I need to go prepare for our trip tomorrow."

"Sure, go ahead," he said, his head spinning from what he had told him.

He turned to leave, but he stopped her.

"Can I walk around?"

"Sure, but you need to rest. You just survived a crash and your foot is broken."

"I'm a tough Marine. I'll suck it up."

He enjoyed the warm morning sun as he walked the more than six-acre property that encompassed the main house compound.

The perimeter was surrounded by an eight-foot fence with large eucalyptus trees every dozen feet and the entrance was fortified with an iron gate.

Roger, Zach, and Steve were busy setting out containers, boxes and packs for their trip. What seemed odd was he wasn't loading any of the vehicles he had housed in the garage, of which two worked. Too curious to let it go, he walked over to them and stopped to ask a few questions.

"Why aren't you loading up the old Suburbans?"

"We're not taking them," Roger answered.

"Oh, so is someone picking you up?"

"Yes, we're being picked up."

"Steve mentioned you're abandoning the house. Does that go for the SUVs?"

"They're yours too if you need them," Roger answered, his attention never leaving the task at hand.

"It's late morning, and I'm starving. Care to join us for a snack?" Roger asked.

"Sure," Vincent said and hobbled along after them as they headed toward the main house.

Inside, Vincent took a seat at the large dinette table opposite Roger. Signs of their impending departure was everywhere. Boxes sat below opened cabinets. The couple of house staff still lingering were placing essential items in each one.

"Where are you going?" Vincent asked, not wasting time with casual chitchat and going right into more questions.

"Ha! Why not at least take a bite of your biscuit before we get into the heavy conversation," Roger quipped.

"Sorry. I've been waiting to ask you since we last talked."

Not looking at Vincent, Roger spread butter on his biscuit and said, "I have a bunker in Colorado. We're going there."

"That's a long drive."

"We're not driving. A couple choppers are coming to pick us up."

"Nice."

"You know there's room for you if you care to join us. Having a Marine bunker down with us could be valuable."

"I don't think I can. I've got to report back to my unit."

"What does that mean, Sergeant Vincent? I'm trying to understand how your mind works. Let me tell you something, I have had access to privileged information for several decades now. I say that because what I'm about to tell you will come as a shock, but the government will not be coming to save anyone. Their contingency in an event like this is to hunker down and allow Americans to rip each other apart. They'll come out of their safe and well-stocked bunkers and clean up the mess afterwards. The government has been the largest prepper in the world. While your fancy elite laugh at their cocktail parties about those who get ready for a day like this, the government's been doing exactly that, but all those supplies, guns, bullets, weapons, food, water, all of it is for them. They don't give two cents about you or me. We have been nothing more than pawns. Oh, yes, I had gained status and rank and was even invited to have a spot years ago in one of those bunkers. Once I saw what they were doing, I followed in their footsteps and got my own. I saw them prepping, so I prepped. I heard about them buying food, I bought food; if I heard about them stockpiling weapons, I stockpiled weapons. I learned a lesson a long time ago, don't listen to people, watch them," he said and took a large bite of his biscuit.

Vincent's jaw just hung open. He wasn't naïve and knew the government had their little caches of equipment and so forth, but to hear a man as accomplished as Roger openly discuss what he knew because he got a glimpse behind the curtain made him feel uneasy and in some ways duped.

The screen door sprang open and in came Miguel, a longtime worker on Roger's property. He was sweating and out of breath.

"We have people at the gate."

"How many this time?" Roger asked.

"Too many to count, they're demanding we give them food. And they're very angry."

Roger wiped his mouth with a napkin and stood up.

Vincent followed, hobbling on one leg until he reached his crutches.

Roger wasted no time leaving the house; he needed to see who was at his gate.

Vincent came out and asked him, "Is there anything I can do?"

"Yes, get your weapons."

Three Miles North of Calexico, CA

Michael woke up quickly, panting and sweating. The sun was beaming directly on him through a small window. The temperature in the little shed had risen to the point it was uncomfortable.

He squinted at the sun and used his hand to cover his eyes. He sat up and stretched. His body still hurt; he feared his aches and pains would be with him for a couple weeks. By how high the sun was in the sky, he guessed it was late morning, and that meant he had slept a very long time.

He needed to get on the road; every minute he was there, he wasn't in San Diego helping his brother. He couldn't fault himself for sleeping; he needed the rest.

Outside, he began his search for fuel; fortunately for him it was easy. Several company trucks had gas; all he needed to do was siphon it.

Working on the fuel issue, he allowed his thoughts to go to the last thing he remembered, Viktor Azamov. He didn't recall who he was specifically, but if they were at war with Russia and there was a Russian on the container ship where the missile was fired from, then there was no doubt the Russians started it with the EMP. Over and over again he saw Viktor's face, a scarred face with a set of half gold teeth. This was a clearer image than he had ever had of someone from the ship. He could see him clearly, talking to him with a thick accent. He now had a memory of Viktor threatening him while he was being tortured.

That memory made him stand up straight. So he was working against Viktor; he was not working for them. Somehow they had found out about him and were torturing him, but why? Why not kill him?

He carried two jugs of gas back to the car and started topping it off when he could quote Viktor during one of the times he was torturing him. *Before you die, just know that I'll kill your pretty Karina. We know where she is and we'll do the worst things you can imagine to her.'* Then a flash and black. That was all he remembered from that moment. Who was Karina? Was that his wife or lover? She must have been special; why else mention her? He struggled to remember. Frustrated, he began to smack himself in the head and cried out, "Think, damn you, remember!" But nothing came.

The only place he kept seeing in his mind was San Diego. So without anything else, he'd have to make San Diego his destination still.

With the Chevette topped off, he was on the road again, a man lost on a lonely road.

Vista, CA

A tall iron gate was the only thing that stood between them and what sounded like dozens of people. From the screams and yelling, Vincent could tell they were not a happy bunch.

Vincent move as fast as the crutches would let him. His injury frustrated him and if he was going to get into a fight having crutches and a broken foot wasn't optimal. Slung over his back was his rifle and his service issued Beretta 92F pistol was tucked in his waistband.

Miguel had parked an old crew cab Chevy truck alongside the gate. This helped block it from being pushed open and gave Roger a platform to engage the angry crowd of people who once were his happy neighbors.

The people outside were begging for him to open the gate and let them in. They were among the hundreds of thousands of San Diegans that were now scavenging and on the hunt for food and a safe place. Things deteriorated quickly, and for his neighbors, they suspected he had plentiful resources because he was wealthy. During times like this, rumors were the only source of information, and rumors locally had spread that Roger had a compound full of food and supplies.

Vincent couldn't make out the back-and-forth between the group and Roger until he reached the truck where Roger stood.

"People, everyone, please stop yelling!" Roger called back to the unruly group. With every surge the gate bowed in and hit the side of the truck Roger was perched on.

"People, please calm down!"

The only response he received was multiple people yelling, "Let us in! We know you have food! We need help!"

Vincent knew what people were capable of when their only choices left were finding food or starving. This situation could easily escalate and spill over into the farm.

Roger's plea for calm wasn't working. These people wanted in. They were in need and desperate.

With everyone's focus on the gate, nobody saw a few in the group climb the fence about thirty feet away.

Vincent turned and saw two men clear the fence and make for the barn.

How was this possible? Vincent thought. The power had only been out for days max? Why were people already resorting to this type of behavior? Vincent dropped his right crutch, grabbed the grip of the pistol in his waistband, and pulled it out. He pointed it at a man who had just cleared the fence and yelled, "Stop. Just stop what you're doing and leave!"

The man stopped instantly and focused on him. He looked middle-aged. Smears of dirt covered their unshaven and darkly tanned faces.

Time slowed down for Vincent like it always did when he was faced with a life-or-death scenario. He had the gun trained on the man closest to him but was looking at each one carefully to see if any of them had a gun.

"Hey, listen, we're hungry. I know he has food, I need to feed my family!" the man said motioning with his arms to the barn, house and farm around him.

"This is not yours. You need to leave now," Vincent firmly ordered.

The man who had spoken looked at the other. They locked eyes and then turned their attention back to Vincent.

Only ten feet at the most separated the man from him. If he ran and climbed back across the fence, Vincent would let him go, but if he took a step toward him, he would have no choice but to shoot.

"Come on, man," the man said.

"I need you two to leave, now!" Vincent said louder.

The tension in the air was thick. The man's hunger and his basic human instincts was telling him not to move. Roger's farm promised survival and he was close to having food.

The sounds around him gave Vincent a picture that things were now collapsing quickly. He needed to do something about the man so he could address the chaos everywhere else.

The man had a pistol tucked in his pants and stupidly he went for it.

Vincent sighted in and squeezed off a round.

The man grunted and collapsed to the ground. Unbeknownst to Vincent, his gunshot was the first in a short but bloody battle that was coming.

Vincent turned to find Roger but he was gone from him perch on the truck. The gate had held but people were now clearing the fence and were running everywhere. At the main house he heard glass breaking followed by more screaming.

Out from behind the guesthouse, Miguel appeared with a shotgun in his hand. He ran towards the people coming over the fence. Fear was written all over him. His head pivoted back and forth. He didn't know what to do, so he freaked out and began shooting people. With the 12-gauge shotgun nestled in his shoulder, he pulled the trigger repeatedly.

The hollering from the invaders turned to screams of horror as they soon realized the mistake of trespassing.

Gunfire suddenly erupted from the main house. Screams of terror soon followed.

With the main house under attack, Vincent turned his attention there.

"Damn it!" he yelled out as he moved as fast as he could referencing his broken and heavily bandaged foot.

Screams and more gunfire reverberated from the main house.

The distance from the barn to the house was only a hundred yards but with his foot it felt like miles.

As he grew closer, some of the invaders came pouring out of the house, their arms full of food and other supplies. Steve bolted out after them armed with a pistol. He leveled the pistol and pulled the trigger hitting a man no older than twenty squarely in the back. He collapsed to the ground; the food and supplies he was carrying spilled out across the lawn. Steve turned towards another man, he again pulled the trigger hitting the him in the chest.

What reluctance Vincent had to shoot these people was evaporated in an instance. After seeing Steve bravely defending himself and his property, he knew the rules had changed, and that he'd better change too. This was about survival, pure and simple. He raised his pistol, and shot a man running by him. He then took aim on another, then pivoted and hit another and another until his magazine emptied. He transitioned to his rifle and continued until he saw no one left standing except for Steve.

Carlsbad, CA

Their morning had been nonstop. First Nicholas asked if Bryn and Sophie would want to come to Montana, that segued into Bryn's confiding a dark secret, and to finish off a somber morning, they buried Matt in the backyard. Now Bryn and Nicholas were preparing their weapons before they headed out to get another vehicle, a trailer for the Bronco, drop off the Dodge and stop by Bryn's old place to get what supplies she had and to invite Colin to join their caravan.

Nicholas thought the morning was tough until Abigail came into the garage.

"Dad, you promised. Please stop by and check on him!" Abigail complained.

"I don't have time, honey. I'm sure he's fine," Nicholas said, his attention more on checking his weapons versus listening to her.

"You promised. I can't leave without knowing he's okay."

"I can't."

"Dad, please!"

Her shriek got his attention. "I'll try."

"You've said that, but each day you don't."

"Who is this boy? Is he your boyfriend?"

Their conversation was occurring in front of Bryn, who tried not to crack a smile. All she could think was girls and their crushes.

"What's the address again?"

"11236 Claremont Boulevard."

"Why are you seeing a boy who lives down there and why are you seeing a boy period? Does your mother know about this? I swear I asked and she doesn't."

"Argh, you make me so mad!" Abigail yelled.

Bryn began to chuckle.

"What's so funny?" Abigail yelled.

Not able to resist, Bryn turned and answered, "This boy you're so consumed with, how old is he. Actually scratch that, it doesn't matter, boys are nothing more than men with more hair, more stamina and less years on this planet. Let me tell you about men, boys, whatever. This boy is probably already fucking some other girl or at least trying to. If he's proclaiming his love for you, it's only so he can screw you."

"Dad, are you going to let her talk to me that way?" Abigail asked, astonished by her comments.

"Well, Abby, I think she nailed it. That was spot on."

"Argh, you don't know Rob. He's not like that!"

Abigail again screamed and stormed away.

Bryn looked at him and said, "I feel so bad that you have to deal with all these hormones while the apocalypse is going on."

Nicholas laughed loudly.

"Guys, hurry, hurry; Brent's leaving with the Bronco!" Alex yelled as he ran into the driveway from the street.

Hearing this, Nicholas and Bryn sprinted out of the garage. They made the street just in time as Brent was driving down it.

Nicholas held his arms in the air and stood directly in front of him.

Brent accelerated but saw that Nicholas wasn't moving. He slammed on the brakes, causing some items improperly secured to the roof to slide off, smashing into the pavement.

"Stop!" Nicholas yelled.

"Get out of the way, Nic. I'm taking the Bronco. I'm leaving with my family. We're going somewhere safe!"

Nicholas could see he wasn't lying. He had the vehicle loaded up and his family inside.

"Brent, we can work this out. We just need to use it one more day, and then you can have it."

"Use that old car. I'm taking this one."

"I can't; it's not mine. I need to return it. Please just get out of the truck. We had a deal.'

"Fuck the deal!"

"Fuck you!" Bryn yelled and pulled out her pistol.

Brent's wife, Evelyn, screamed when she saw the pistol.

A voice from the backseat called out, "Everyone calm down!"

"Chandler, is that you?" Nicholas asked.

His arm jutted out the driver's window and waved.

"You're leaving too?"

"It's not safe; we're going to my sister's place in Big Bear."

"And taking the truck? Aren't you a lying sack of shit!" Nicholas hollered. "I've had enough; get out of the fucking truck now!"

"No!"

Becky, Abigail and Sophie had heard the commotion and came out to see what was going on.

"Nic, what's going on?"

"Go back inside," he ordered Becky and Abigail.

"Bryn, I've got the front. Go to the driver's side and get the keys," Nicholas said as he pulled out his pistol and pointed it at Brent.

Bryn did as he said and walked around to the driver's door.

Brent reached up and locked it.

She raised her pistol and said, "Give me the keys and get fucking out!"

Evelyn screamed, and with a fight or flight reaction, she pushed down on Brent's right leg, forcing his foot into the accelerator.

The Bronco lunged forward at a high rate of speed.

Becky screamed and rushed Nicholas. She pushed him clear, but the Bronco rammed her and the force of the impact tossed her ten feet. She hit the pavement with a hard thud, her head making the worst contact of all.

Nicholas picked himself up, turned and saw Becky lying on the ground unconscious.

Screaming came from inside and outside the vehicle.

Abigail ran to her mother. "Mom, no!"

Brent stopped but soon realized there was nothing they could do. He hit the gas again, this time on his own. The Bronco spun tires and sped off down the street.

Nicholas ran to Becky's side. He checked her pulse and breathed easier when he found it.

Bryn wanted to shoot the Bronco but hesitated for fear of damaging it. However, after seeing what Brent had just done, she saw red. Brent was just another bully, and she wasn't going to allow him to get away with it. She sprinted for the Dodge, jumped in, started it and tore out of the driveway in pursuit of Brent.

She made the first right turn at more than fifty miles an hour and in ten seconds had cleared the gate, which Brent had conveniently left opened for her. Pulling up to the main road, she looked left and right and in the distance spotted the red Bronco to her right. She tore out of the community's entrance and weaved in and around all the cars.

Brent was driving conservatively and didn't see Bryn closing in until she was on him.

She hit the gas pedal and jumped the sidewalk and sped down it past the Bronco. Seeing a break in the cars, she turned the car hard to the left, cutting him off.

Brent had two choices, run into her or veer the truck into the oncoming lanes. Not wanting to ram her, he jerked the wheel hard to the left and into the other lanes. Trying to avoid a stalled car, he turned the wheel hard to the right, but the front left of the Bronco clipped the car. This almost caused him to lose control.

Frustrated that she couldn't stop him, she tried harder, but now her rage was turning to reason. If she caused him to crash, she could lose the Bronco and possibly kill innocent people. She also risked crashing the Dodge, and if that happened, they'd be out of the only operational car they had. As reason began to win out, she slowed down and eventually pulled the car over. Her arm throbbed with pain and her heart raced. She wanted nothing more than to beat Brent to a pulp but that wasn't going to happen. Accepting this fact, she watched Brent and her beautiful truck disappear over the hill.

El Centro, CA

The name Karina kept ringing in his head. He focused intently on the name until he could see her face or what he imagined her face might look like. Was that it? He thought. Were these nothing but visions or thoughts, or were they actual memories?

He was beyond frustrated. He wanted his memory back, because without it, who was he? How could one have a life if they didn't know who they were? This is where he hoped his brother could help; Nicholas could be that person who could confirm parts of his past so he didn't have to doubt the *memories*.

Interstate 8 was just ahead. A simple turn to the left took him west towards San Diego and his brother. He headed for the exit, but then his eyes took him to the sign that read PHOENIX. He took notice that he was drawn to it, but refocused on the Interstate 8 West sign.

He couldn't shake the odd feeling about seeing the sign for Phoenix. Was this a telltale memory coming back or a false positive? He pulled off the road and slammed the car into park.

Right took him to Phoenix, his guts said go there, but the logical part of his brain told him to go west.

It didn't make any sense to go to Phoenix, or did it?

"Stick with the plan," he said.

He put the car into drive and headed for the Interstate 8 West exit, he consciously kept his eyes glued to the West sign. "No more distraction, stay focused." In his peripheral vision he could see the Phoenix sign, but with all his might he stayed true and passed it.

His body instinctually put on his blinker, causing him to laugh. How funny it was to follow all the old rituals and rules when it didn't matter anymore. With his eyes intently focused on the exit, he lost sight of his surroundings and his situational awareness.

The truck slammed into him going about fifty miles an hour. It struck the rear driver's side, forcing the little Chevette to spin several times before coming to a rest under the freeway right next to the on-ramp.

The force of the impact didn't knock him out, but he was dazed. He unfastened the seat belt and crawled out the window only to fall to the pavement in a pool of shattered glass.

The sound of grinding glass and pavement hit his ears. He looked up and saw a blur of two people walking towards him. About to lose consciousness, he rolled onto his back. He didn't know how much more abuse his body could take, but Michael McNeil was not an easy man to kill and many had tried.

A man bent down and smacked Michael's face. "Mikhail, wake up."

"Huh, what?"

The other person spoke; a woman. "His name isn't Mikhail, it's Michael." She bent down and caressed his bleeding face. "Michael, sweetheart, it's Karina. Where do you think you're going?"

He opened his eyes and saw the face he had envisioned. He reached up towards her, but she stopped him.

"Michael, it's time to come home," she said.

Those were the last words he heard before passing out.

CHAPTER 5

"All changes are more or less tinged with melancholy, for what we are leaving behind is part of ourselves." – Amelia Barr

Vista, CA

The battle at the ranch had been more intense than anything Vincent had seen in Afghanistan. Sure, his combat tours had their moments, but what happened yesterday was shocking. What others, neighbors and friends, were willing to do for a slice of bread, and what he was willing to do himself. He had lost a part of himself yesterday, and he didn't think he'd be able to get it back.

The long night offered him a chance to reassess his life and where things were going in the country. His concern for his parents still ate at him, and if he went back to his unit, to his Marines, he didn't know when or if he'd ever get a chance to ensure they were safe. When he laid his head down to sleep the night before, he gave himself permission to explore the possibility of not returning to his unit. He kept his mind open, and if he woke feeling the same way, he'd do just that, but if he woke with any reservations at all, he'd take one of the SUVs and drive directly to Camp Pendleton.

As if God or some higher being was guiding him, he had woken unchanged. He had been given another lease on life after the helicopter crash, and if he was ever going to be there for his parents, now was the time. Roger had been hurt during the fighting, but it didn't stop him from getting his family ready for their departure. He again offered Vincent a seat on the chopper and a place in his bunker if he wanted it.

"Sergeant, I hate to leave you in your condition. You do know you're more than welcome to come. Please, we have the space and plenty of resources. You'd be welcome."

"I'll be fine plus I've made up my mind. I'm going to Idaho to check on my parents, but if something comes up, can I come later?"

"Of course."

Vincent nodded. "Thank you for saving me."

"Thank you for helping us yesterday. That was quite a struggle," Roger said holding up his bandaged arm.

"Can I be blunt?"

"Sure."

"You all fought, I didn't think you'd do that. You struck me as a man of peace."

Roger placed his good hand on Vincent's shoulder and said, "I am a man of peace but I won't let people just come and take what they want. I taught my kids to defend themselves. I may regret some of the things I did in the past, but don't mistake past regrets and a renewed obligation to doing what is right with allowing others to harm you. I believe in helping others but I will never stand by and let others harm my family."

Vincent nodded and now felt a bit silly for asking. Of course this man he barely knew would protect his family. He just sized him up quickly that he would never use deadly force. Maybe those people felt that way too and judged him wrong.

Roger was an intriguing man, if he wasn't heading back to Idaho, he would definitely join him wherever he was going.

"You sure you don't want to come with us?" Roger asked.

"I'm sure for now."

Roger held up his finger and said, "Give me a minute." He walked into the house and reemerged a few minutes later. "Take this," he said handing Vincent a business card.

"Okay," Vincent said and looked at it. Roger's name was on it and below he had hand written in a long ten digit phone number.

"It's my satellite phone number. Call me if we can help."

"I don't have a phone."

"Yes you do, I left a case for you, in it you'll find one as well as an assortment of other things."

"I don't know what to say."

"Thank you for yesterday and for all the service you've ever given this nation. It's the least I can do."

"Thank you, sir. So when are the choppers coming?"

Like clockwork the heavy thump of two helicopters bounced off the house.

They both looked and he spotted them first. Two Sikorsky S-76 helicopters flew over and circled back around.

"You guys definitely do things in style."

"No reason not to, but this is more about safety then style," Roger commented.

The helicopters landed on the rear lawn. Immediately the crew and one staff person from Roger's bunker jumped out and met Steve.

"I have to go," Roger said and turned. "Goodbye, Sergeant Vincent," he said and hurried off.

"Goodbye, Roger and thanks for the house," he joked.

The crew wasted no time loading up their belongings, and within minutes of landing they were whisked away.

Vincent covered his eyes so he could watch them as long as possible until they were mere specks in the sky. He turned and looked at the house, his house for all intents and purposes. He'd rest up a few more days and then head north. He didn't know what he'd encounter on the road, but there wasn't any doubt he'd meet some interesting people along the way.

Carlsbad, CA

"Please tell me she'll be fine?" Nicholas said his eyes showing the strain of seeing that his wife may not survive.

"Nic, I'm doing everything I can, but right now, I feel

227

confident she'll be okay. I need her to rest."

"What can I do?"

Proctor looked at his old friend and knew the best thing for him was to stay busy. Having Nicholas pacing the bedroom or the halls of the house would only distract him and the place Nicholas was needed was out trying to find another vehicle and gathering more supplies.

"I need you to go prep for our departure."

Nicholas looked down in frustration that he couldn't do something to make her wake up. Having to wait was not his strong suit and there wasn't any amount of money or focus he could expend that would change it.

"Fine, but she's in your hands. Tell Abigail to do whatever you ask."

After Becky's accident, Nicholas dispatched Bryn to Proctor's and had him brought immediately. However, Proctor wasn't coming without his family and upon seeing them all, Nicholas felt better. This meant Proctor would be able to give Becky round the clock care.

"I'll be fine, I have more than enough help," Proctor said referring to Abigail, his wife Katherine and Sophie.

Nicholas looked past him to Becky. Her body lay so sweetly on the bed, her arms crossed over her belly and her chest rising slowly with each breath. "You're right I need to go get a car or two." He walked to the side of the bed and sat down. Gently he picked up her hand and with extra care gave it a kiss. Whispering, he said, "You get well, Proctor and the others will take care of you. I'll be back soon." He put her hand back and stood, but before he walked away he leaned back over her and gave her a kiss on the forehead. "I love you, baby."

Proctor watched Nicholas' display of love and felt a tug of emotion. He cared for both of these people and seeing her like she was and Nicholas in pain hurt him too.

"Thanks buddy," Nicholas said giving Proctor a quick hug.

In the hall Nicholas was stopped abruptly by Abigail; "How's Mom?"

"Hi, sweetie."

"Is she going to live?"

Nicholas pulled her close and said, "Of course she is. Don't say that. Your mother will be fine. I need you to help Proctor do whatever he asks."

"Where are you going?"

"I need to go find another car but before I do that I need to gather your grandparents. They need to know what happened."

"Can you check on Rob?"

"I don't have time for this guy. Haven't I told you this is not a good time?" he said kissing her on the cheek.

Abigail barked, "Dad, you promised!"

He hurried down the stairs towards the living room. Watching him, she grew angry, her fist clenched, and she slammed the wall.

Proctor stepped out of the master bedroom to see what banged on the wall. He saw Abigail standing there, her body rigid and shoulders slumped forward.

"Abby, is everything okay?"

She craned her head and snapped, "My dad's just an asshole is all." She stormed off to her bedroom and slammed the door.

"Rifle?" Nicholas asked.

"Check," Bryn answered.

"Shotgun?"

"I got it," Alex replied, admiring the wooden stock of the Remington.

"Everyone checked the pistols and you all have extra magazines?" Nicholas asked.

"Yes, sir," Bryn joked.

"Take this shit seriously. You know how bad it is out there," Nicholas said.

"Oh, I know."

"How's your arm?" Alex asked as he stowed the shotgun in the backseat of the Dodge.

"Hurts a bit but that's what pain killers are for," Bryn smiled.

"You let me know if you need a shoulder massage or anything," Alex joked.

"Aren't you married? And second, you're like ancient."

"A guy gets a few gray hairs and everyone thinks he's old as dirt."

"You are old as dirt, I know because I am," Nicholas said, tossing in a back-pack next to the shotgun.

Bryn got into the car and hollered, "If you ladies are done chit-chatting can we get going?"

Nicholas stared at Bryn; he liked her a lot. She was tough and ready for whatever. The chase she gave Brent was inspiring, but he was happy to know she hadn't taken it to the point of destroying both vehicles.

Nicholas and Alex climbed in and set off for another day of car hunting.

No matter the smiles or jokes Nicholas told as they headed out the gates and into the unknown, he couldn't get Becky out of his mind. If she were to die from her injuries he'd be lost without her. So far he felt he was batting five hundred, he needed to improve his stats or they wouldn't survive.

San Diego, CA

Nicholas pulled the Dodge into Sycamore Grove and parked it next to Bryn's Kia. Frustrated, he slammed the gear shift into park and rested into the vinyl seats.

"Tomorrow, we have tomorrow," Bryn said.

Alex got out, shotgun in hand, and looked around.

A few people came out of the apartments and looked at them. Seeing an operational vehicle was becoming a rarity, so when one pulled into the complex they had to see what was going on.

"How many tomorrows do we have?" Nicholas lamented.

"As many as it takes. You have this old ride, that's something."

"Speaking of that, I need to go get my in laws today, I have to."

"We will. It won't take us long here and we'll be on our

way. Hey, we did find a trailer, that's something positive."

"It was like a no-brainer when we pulled in there," Nicholas said, referring to the U-Haul rental lot they had visited earlier.

Bryn looked outside and said, "We have a couple more hours, plenty of time."

Nicholas' stress was mainly coming from concern for Becky. He couldn't stand not knowing her condition. The luxury of mobile phones and easy communication was taken for granted. He thought about the times he'd turned off his phone because he found it a burden; now he wished he had one that worked.

Bryn got out and slammed the car door. She holstered her pistol and tucked her t-shirt into her jeans. The few people who were on their balconies looking she recognized but there was something new about them, a look that told her they were becoming desperate.

"Let's just drive the old Dodge right up to my place, I don't think we need to worry about the landscaping anymore," Bryn said.

"Yeah, that's a good idea," Alex replied.

Nicholas didn't comment. He started the car back up and pulled it up onto the sidewalk and followed slowly behind Bryn as she casually guided him between two buildings. When she cleared the corner her body tensed. She expected to run into the three amigos but surprisingly it was quiet.

A familiar puff of smoke floated from the second-floor landing. "I was wondering what happened to you!" Colin said, sitting in his chair hidden behind the railing.

"Colin!"

He stood and looked down on her with a smile, "Yes ma'am."

"I'm so happy you're okay."

"Of course I am. Who are your friends?"

"A couple guys who saved me and Sophie."

"Saved, hmm, did you get into some trouble out there?" he asked, moving to the top of the stairs.

"Yeah, just a bit, I'm, um, running with these guys now. This is Nicholas and this is Alex," she said pointing at each one.

Nicholas parked the car and got out just in time for her to introduce him. He looked at Colin and waved.

Alex nodded, but his attention was on the buildings and odd people he saw milling around.

"You have good timing," Colin said.

She ran up the stairs and said, "We came to grab my stuff."

"Where are your compatriots?" he asked.

She was standing in front of him now, a painful look told him something bad had occurred.

"Who?" he asked.

"Matt, he's…"

Colin knew what she was attempting to say but couldn't. "I'm sorry."

"Hey, can we hurry up?" Nicholas said jogging up the stairs.

Bryn snapped out of her emotional state and headed for her apartment door.

"Colin, nice to meet you," Nicholas said, putting his

hand out.

"Hi, Nicholas, right?"

"Yeah, um, we are short on time and I don't like to be running around at night."

"Understand," Colin nodded, stuffing his cigar between his teeth.

Bryn had gained access and quickly turned around with an arm full.

"Here, let me help you," Nicholas said, concerned about her arm.

"Oh, she's tough," Colin joked.

"It's not that; she was shot."

Bryn rushed down the stairs and put the items in the trunk.

"Where?"

"Arm," Nicholas answered as he shuffled past carrying three cases of bottled water.

"Girl, are you doing all right?" Colin asked as he began to help.

"I'm good and thanks for helping."

All three loaded everything she and the others had collected. It filled the trunk with only a few items having to go into the back seat.

She stood looking into her darkened apartment. Sadness gripped her as she realized this would be the last time she'd see it. So much had happened in such a short period of time.

The sweet smell from Colin's cigar hit her nostrils. She turned and came right out with it. "Colin, we want you to come with us. It's dangerous out there and we could use someone like you."

"Me?"

"Yeah, I talked it over with Nic. He's cool, you'll like him."

Colin shrugged his massive shoulders and cocked his head, "Oh, I don't know. I'm kind of a lone wolf."

"Lone wolves don't last long, no matter how strong they are," Nicholas interjected, his shadow casting long into the apartment.

Colin turned and looked at him. "You don't me and I don't know you."

"Bryn's told me enough. We need good people and I hear you were in the Navy."

"She's a good girl but let's be honest, you don't know me either," Colin said to Bryn.

She stepped towards him and said in a gentle voice, "I have a good sense about people and while I foolishly lived my life before in a blur of devices and parties I have come to see people for who they are. Nic and his family and friends are good people and so are you. No one does what you did, I was in need and you helped without asking. Good people do that."

"You don't know my past," he replied, a look of shame on his face.

"I don't know what you're referring to but if you did something stupid in your past that's your past," Bryn said

"I don't know, your invite is nice, but I don't know."

"Colin, do you care to tell me why you don't think you're worthy?" Nicholas asked.

"It's not that, well, maybe it is. I just don't trust

people," Colin answered.

Almost at the same time both Bryn and Nicholas said, "I don't either." They laughed and Nicholas kept talking. "Colin, whatever it is, Bryn sees a good man and we need more good people in our group. I intend on surviving this and I can only do that with others."

Colin turned his gaze from Nicholas to Bryn and before he could respond a shot cracked loudly from outside.

Nicholas turned around and looked over the railing, his pistol now drawn.

Alex stood, a blank stare on his face.

"Alex!" Nicholas hollered.

The shotgun fell from Alex's grip and hit the ground. He followed and dropped to his knees and fell over.

From Nicholas' perspective he couldn't tell if he was dead or not, but it didn't look promising because he didn't move.

Colin ran out of the apartment, a pistol in his grip. He took cover behind the railing and peered over.

Bryn used the doorway to give her cover and also tried to get a view of who had taken the shot.

Nicholas' instincts overcame any fears he might have felt. He sprinted down the stairs towards Alex's still body.

He had mentioned before how there were only three types of people in the world, those who ran towards danger, those who ran from it and those who froze. Years before in Kuwait when he saw firsthand how men killed each other, he didn't hesitate then; he ran towards the danger and his bravery resulted in him getting wounded. He didn't give his actions any thought then and didn't give them any thought now. His friend was down and he needed to help.

More gun-fire cracked, with one bullet ricocheting off an air-conditioning unit next to the bottom of the stairs where he had just been.

This close call told him that whoever was shooting had him in their crosshairs.

Like a baseball player hoping to be safe at home plate, he slid hard into Alex who didn't respond.

"Alex!" Nicholas cried.

With no response and a blood soaked shirt with the bullet hole centered on his back, Nicholas knew the shot was probably fatal.

Nicholas ducked when two shots hit the Dodge just to his right.

"Where are they?" Nicholas cried out.

The additional gun-fire was all Colin needed. He homed in and found the source, a small downstairs window in an adjacent building.

"Bryn the building ahead, lower right window, fire on it!" Colin ordered.

Bryn didn't argue. She stepped out, took aim and began to squeeze off rounds.

Colin began engaging the window and called out to Nicholas, "Building ahead of you, lower right window!"

Nicholas picked up the shotgun and yelled, "Cover me!" He ran towards the apartment building. The cover fire from Colin and Bryn did exactly what he needed it to do. Whoever had engaged him was no longer firing and, by his guess, had taken cover. He cleared the forty feet and slammed his back against the wall. Nicholas signaled for them to stop firing.

The complex fell silent.

Inside the first-floor apartment Nicholas could hear several unintelligible voices. He could tell they sounded distressed but couldn't make out what they were saying.

Nicholas pressed himself against the stucco wall and his eyes were on the window six feet away.

The voices grew louder and he made out there were three people, all male.

He had made it this far, but he didn't have a plan, and just what he was he going to do next was vexing him until he saw the barrel of a rifle nudge out the window. Not waiting to formulate, he was going to at least take one person out. He pivoted out and swung the shotgun around until the window and the man just inside came into full view. He pulled the trigger of the 12 gauge. A powerful blast of double ought buck exited the barrel and slammed into the man. He pumped the action of the shotgun and again pulled the trigger, no visible target was in his sight just a hope that there was.

Loud footfalls from behind startled him; he swung his shotgun towards the sound but stopped when he saw it was Colin and Bryn.

Colin's movements were agile and swift for a man of his size. He ran up to the front door of the apartment and kicked it. The door exploded open.

Yells came from inside then several gunshots.

Bryn entered the darkness of the apartment right behind Colin. When her eyes adjusted to the limited light she saw a gruesome sight. On the living room floor was Craig, he had taken a bullet to his head. Crawling away in agonizing pain was Alberto.

Colin had hit him once in the stomach and his third shot had only grazed his shoulder.

Bryn walked over to him and stepped on his leg.

Alberto cried out in pain and rolled onto his back. He looked into Bryn's face and with terror on his face pleaded, "Please don't kill me."

Nicholas rushed into the room and surveyed the carnage.

"You killed my friend," Bryn barked.

Alberto held up his arms, his hands trembling. "Please no. It wasn't me."

"What you going to do?" Colin asked.

"He can't live," Bryn stated flatly.

"No, please, it wasn't me," Alberto begged.

"Nic, thoughts?" Colin asked.

"Bryn's right, he can't live, he has to pay for Alex."

Colin nodded and said, "I'll do it. I shot him already, let me finish him."

Alberto's frantic eyes darted around the room. He was hoping to find mercy in one of the three.

"Please, no, don't do this; you don't have to do this."

Bryn raised her pistol until the front sight lined up with his face.

Using his hands as a shield, Alberto cried, "Please."

"Bryn no need for you to get your hands dirty like this," Colin said.

She looked over at him and replied, "I don't have a

problem with this. He's evil, you know that. He's a savage and will only find another person to torment or hurt. This is justice." She turned her attention back to Alberto and pulled the trigger.

The confrontation had been a surprise but not unexpected. This was becoming the new norm for them. The EMP had not only removed all critical infrastructures, it had decimated society. Its true effect was still unfolding, but the veneer that had held everything together had been ripped off. With the inability of law enforcement or military to respond, a power vacuum was created and lawlessness took hold. Laws worked when people obeyed them; many did so because the fear of consequence was a restraint. That was gone, and with it civility.

Nicholas knew this and so did Bryn. They would have to be judge and jury until some sort of order was restored. But what nagged at them both was they feared order wouldn't return soon, so in its absence and for their own safety, they'd have to take out the trash, so to speak. One thing he wasn't expecting to see, especially from Bryn, was her ability to compartmentalize and do what he described as the heavy lifting. To look at her you'd think she was a small, cute woman. Maybe he had prejudices built in him that made it hard to look at a woman as someone who would take deliberate even vicious action. He couldn't see Becky being this way nor could he imagine Abigail. However, the story she shared earlier and her life experiences made her unforgiving of men specifically those who hurt people. He didn't want to dwell on it too much, but he couldn't help but look at her differently than the other women in his life. Bryn was unique, that was for sure.

The conflict at Sycamore Grove was enough for Colin to make up his mind. He agreed to come with them and his acceptance proved to be critical to accumulating the assets they needed to make the trip.

Stored in his garage was the one item they desperately needed, a vehicle. But this wasn't just any vehicle, it was a 1968 Chevy Suburban. It had been his mother's, and after her death he had brought it back from Louisiana.

Nicholas couldn't believe their luck. In fact, after the events of the day he thought it wasn't luck but divine intervention. It validated what he was doing. His old beliefs that his success was built upon his own abilities ended, he realized that he couldn't succeed in this new world without cooperation and a solid team of people. He had lost Alex but had gained Colin, more equipment and an operational vehicle.

They took another hour to load all of Colin's belongings in the SUV and wrapped Alex's body to transport back home. In as many days they'd be having another funeral. Not only was fighting the new norm but the tragic results of it were also a new norm that he'd have to get used to. After loading Alex's body into the SUV, he paused and reflected on his family. He was doing everything he could to take care of his family's physical safety and health, but was he doing enough for them emotionally. At first he dismissed this thought then he saw Abigail's face and the anger she held towards him because he wouldn't take the time to check on Rob. These thoughts of family soon transitioned to his in-laws. How were they getting along? He had taken his car and was now late in returning it. He had to go get them today, but before he could do that, he needed to fulfill a promise to Abigail.

Bryn didn't agree with Nicholas' decision to go alone to Rob's house, but he insisted. He gave them specific instructions to go back with the SUV. He had secured a second vehicle and didn't want to lose it as soon as he'd gotten it. His sojourn would take time and driving at night was risky.

Bryn had been correct; the address Abigail had given him was a short distance away. When he pulled up outside, he played out what he was going to say. He didn't know how it would be received but he didn't care.

Carrying his rifle and with his pistol holstered, he started to walk to the front door. He stopped halfway and looked down. Was the rifle too much? It would be for him. If a strange man showed up with a rifle slung, he just might shoot him before asking questions. He went back to the car and dropped it off, but kept his pistol.

Once at the front door, he noticed the blinds on the large window next to the door moved.

He banged on the door and stepped aside.

Shuffling and chatter came from the other side.

"I'm here to see Rob Robles. This is Nicholas McNeil, Abigail's father."

More unintelligible chatter.

"Rob and Abigail are dating, I'm here on Abigail's behalf."

The sound of the deadbolt disengaging drew his hands to his pistol.

The door creaked and a face appeared.

"I'm Nicholas McNeil," he said to the woman.

The door opened more to show a woman in her mid forties, "Who are you?" She asked apprehensively unsure she should be talking to this man much less opening her door to an armed man. She took notice of the pistol on his hip

"I'm Nicholas, Nicholas McNeil."

"I heard that, who *are* you?"

"I'm Abigail McNeil's' father."

"Who?"

"Rob is dating my daughter."

Her brows came together and her eyes looked up as she struggled to remember the name.

"Mom, I know who he is," a male voice said from deeper inside the house.

"You know this man?" she asked.

"No, but Abigail is my girlfriend."

"You didn't tell me you had a girlfriend, much less a white girl," she said, astonished and aggravated at just discovering this information.

"I know how you feel," Nicholas said.

Rob came to the door. He was about five foot nine inches tall, dark hair, olive skin and dark brown eyes.

"Hi, I'm Rob. How's Abby?"

"Abby's fine. She asked me to check on you."

"Is she with you?" he asked.

"No, she's home."

"Oh."

Nicholas looked left and right at the houses lining the perfectly straight street. The rumble of his car had drawn attention, and those curious eyes were now outside looking at him and the car. The last thing he needed was another fight over his car.

"Hey, I know me stopping out of the blue seems odd, but I made her a promise," Nicholas said.

"Is that it?" the woman asked. She turned to Rob and said something in Spanish that Nicholas didn't understand.

"Since you asked, yes, that's about it. I promised I'd check on you and let you know she's fine. How are you making out?"

"Good, now goodbye," the woman said and began to close the door.

Rob put his hand out and stopped her, "Don't be like that, Mama."

She gave him a hard look and snapped, "I don't know what you were doing with this man's daughter, but it's over. We are going to your aunt Teresa's place in Texas."

"You have a car that works?" Nicholas asked.

She looked at him with hesitation.

"Yes," Rob answered.

She slapped Rob and said, "Goodbye, Mr. McNeil." The door slammed shut and the deadbolt reengaged.

Nicholas laughed and hoped his risky visit would be enough to satisfy Abigail. Walking back to his car, he came to the realization it wouldn't. She wasn't only female, she was young; those were two things that for him almost certainly guaranteed an emotional and irrational response.

He got back in and started the car. One more stop, his in-laws. He put the car in gear and turned the wheel when a slapping on the side window jarred him.

His hand grasped his pistol and he looked to see Rob frantic. "Mr. McNeil, Mr. McNeil!"

Nicholas rolled the window down and asked, "What?"

"Take me with you. I don't want to go to Texas."

"Um, I don't think that's going to happen."

"Listen, please. I love your daughter. I don't want to lose her."

Nicholas could see the need in his eyes.

"I can't take you away from your parents, so no."

"I'll be eighteen in three months; I can make decisions for myself."

"Well maybe in three months but now, no."

"Mr. McNeil, please."

The front door opened and Rob's mother stepped out with a rifle in her hands.

"Uh, please step away from the car. I can tell that your mother's not in agreement with your plan."

"Get back inside, Roberto, now!"

"Sorry, kid. I'll let Abigail know you love her, though," Nicholas said as he rolled up the window. He sped off down the street. In his rear view mirror he saw Rob watching him, defeat written in his face and hunched shoulders.

Today was becoming one interesting engagement after another. If he had suddenly met his daughter's Hispanic secret boyfriend before the lights went out he'd have some serious words for her and there would be consequences, but now it just didn't seem to matter to him. When he thought about how he would have felt before he questioned his own narrow minded thoughts then. Why would it matter to the Nicholas before if her boyfriend had been Hispanic or come from a family with less means? Did it really? Wasn't he just being like his father-in-law in some ways, bigoted towards a young man who he imagined could never take care of his daughter? When he entered Becky's life he had been a wounded vet without a degree but with a motivation and determined vision to create something greater than he had been given. How could he then look at that young man and have those same thoughts? Was it a natural protection mechanism that all parents were given? Was it in his DNA? He didn't know Rob; he just thought he knew who he was. How ignorant.

The sun was now gone and the intense dark had descended over the highway. The old Dodge had been a Godsend but Nicholas couldn't help but complain at the insufficient light the headlights emitted. Driving was difficult and slow as he had to carefully weave around and avoid debris and abandoned cars. His hands had a white knuckle grip on the steering wheel. He leaned forward, his body tense and his eyes intently scanning the edges of the darkness. He hated that he was out traveling the roads in the dark. The dangers of the world had grown and the violent confrontations were only going to get worse, but he was sure what he had experienced was just the tip of the iceberg.

He prayed that Frank would listen, somewhere deep inside the man a practical side had to reside. He didn't want Frank to listen and come, he needed him to. Becky would wake and she would want him to be there. No matter how frustrating Frank could be or how silly his ways were, he was still her father and they had a bond that was impossible to break. Maybe Becky's injuries would be the catalyst for him to come and once there he could then enlist him to be a part of his group.

The thought of his *group* brought a smile to his face because he was proud of what he had done. They were definitely a motley crew, but each one had something special about them, all talented in their own way. Bryn was strong and a fighter, Sophie was tender and nurturing, Colin, well, he thought, he would represent wisdom, Proctor had skills that were critical, and then there was Abigail. He even began to think of her as a part of this. She was smart, but soon he would discover what talents she brought to the table of survival.

The exit was fast approaching. He was now minutes away from sitting down with Frank. This had to work. He didn't know what skill set he brought to the table, but once Becky woke up, she would not be the same without them there. Then there was Becky; he needed her more than just the love she provided him. She was strong and provided a temperament he didn't have. She had a way about her, an innate ability to communicate, and she'd be invaluable in keeping their group together.

JOHN W. VANCE

He pulled up to Frank and Marjory's condo and parked. Inside he saw candles flickering. He sank into the seat and exhaled loudly. It didn't matter whether he went up now or in five minutes, so he took some time to collect his thoughts and envision how this conversation would go. He imagined sitting them down and telling them about Becky's condition. They'd be upset and demand to see her, he knew this; and then he'd explain the world again and ask them to gather their things because they'd never be coming back. He imagined them complying without issue. He took a deep breath and let it out slowly.

A tap on the window jarred him. He sat up and looked out.

It was Frank.

He opened the door and asked, "Frank, what are you doing out?"

"Never mind that, where have you been with my car?" Frank asked.

"It's a long story, but I have something to tell you."

The light from Frank's flashlight lit the scene. Nicholas could see Frank's bloodshot eyes and the look on his face was different. He looked worried, or was he just tired?

"Come inside. Let's talk," Frank said.

Nicholas got out and together they headed towards the front door.

Frank stopped him, put his arm around him and said, "I'm sorry."

Stunned, Nicholas asked, "For what?"

"I was angry you hadn't shown up with my old Dodge, so I walked to the store. Well, let's say my eyes are open.

248

You were right and I was wrong, and for that I'm sorry. I can be a stubborn old asshole, I know this. I guess getting old has been difficult for me. I don't like it, I want to challenge everything, especially young strong men like you."

"There's nothing young about me anymore."

Frank cocked his head and said, "Would you just shut up for a minute. I'm trying to be contrite here."

Nicholas nodded and allowed Frank to continue.

After a few minutes of confessing why he acted the way he did and had over the years they finished the short distance to the house.

Nicholas now stopped him before walking in. "Um, thank you for that."

"Don't think I won't still be an asshole here or there, I've done it for so long it's a hard habit to break."

Frank patted him on the back, opened the door and asked, "So what's so important?"

CHAPTER 6

"Coming together is a beginning; keeping together is progress and working together is progress." – Henry Ford

Carlsbad, CA
Several Days Later

When Becky opened her eyes, she thought she was dreaming. Surrounding her she saw more than Nicholas and Abigail. Familiar faces smiled down on her. First she saw her mother and father, then she saw Proctor and his wife. There was Bryn and Sophie, and a few faces she didn't know. A tall large black man and a young Hispanic boy were hovering in the back.

"Nic, am I dead?" she asked.

"No, sweetheart, you're not," he answered her, his hand in hers.

"What's going on? Why is everyone standing over me, and who's the gigantic black man?"

Nicholas laughed out loud and turned to Proctor. "Is it the drugs?"

"Probably," Proctor answered.

She tried to sit up, but her head felt heavy and vertigo set in. "I don't feel so good."

"I can attest that this is the best you've been in days," Nicholas said.

"Days?"

"Honey, you've been out for a few days."

"All I remember is I pushed you out of the way and I got hit by the truck."

"Yep, you were knocked out cold. Proctor recommended we sedate you for a bit to help reduce any swelling you might have in your head. You took a hard blow to the noggin."

She leaned in and whispered, "Why is everyone here?"

Nicholas turned and asked, "Do you mind? I want to have some privacy."

Everyone cleared out of the room.

When the door closed, he turned and explained everything that had happened over the past few days.

"I brought Proctor over here as soon as I could. He was so concerned for you, and shit had really gotten bad, so I had him and his family move in here so he could monitor you closely. While you were under, I brought your parents here too. As soon as they heard you were hurt, they came, no complaints. They dropped everything and came with me. Getting Frank out of the damn condo was the best thing for him. "

Becky laughed.

"Taking advantage of your downtime, we went looking for more vehicles. Well, lo and behold, when we went to check on Bryn's friend Colin, we found out he had an old Chevy suburban that ran. Well, of course Abigail wouldn't stop talking about this Rob kid, so I went to go check on him. Long story short he showed up here yesterday. I'll let her explain that in greater detail, but he's here to stay too."

"Wait a minute. Abigail has a boyfriend, and he now lives here? I have died, but I think I've gone to hell."

"I would say it gets worse, but that's about it. We've collected quite a menagerie of people. We're all motivated and ready to fight for our survival. None of these people are quitters. We will not give in; we will defy the odds and make it through this," Nicholas said proudly.

"You make it sound like they're superheroes or something."

"We definitely put up a good fight." Nicholas laughed.

"Great, I've been out cold for mere days and my husband has turned our house into a den of misfits."

"I prefer superheroes, the defiant few. Hey, I like that."

"My head is hurting from all this talk. Maybe I'll go to sleep and wake up to find my husband not this madman who has to be the most optimistic and positive man ever to come out of the apocalypse."

He leaned in and gave her a kiss. "Get some rest. I need you ready for the long trip."

"So we're leaving?"

"You wanted to; that plan hasn't changed. We're all just waiting for you to wake up."

"Montana?"

"Yep, Montana, we leave when you're ready."

She patted him on the hand, and just before she dozed off, she said, "Love you."

"I love you too," he said and kissed her hand. When he closed the door to the bedroom, the laughter and chatter of his eclectic group resonated off the walls.

More than a week had gone by since the EMP hit and the power went out. His group was still unaware that six cities had been destroyed and that the United States had been not only plunged into darkness but into war. Forces greater than them were on the move, and soon they'd come face to face.

He knew the road ahead would be tough and on that road they'd lose a few. He was prepared to tackle any obstacle, but what was coming at him he never would have imagined.

EPILOGUE

Outside Oklahoma City, Texas Federation

Alexis sat glued to every word and name her mother told her, just waiting to hear about the man who would eventually become her biological father.

"That's it for tonight, Lex. I'm tired."

"No, you haven't gotten to the part about my dad."

"Tomorrow, I promise."

"No, please, come on."

"Tomorrow, it's late and I'm tired."

"Can I at least see a picture of him?"

"Sure," Abigail said and walked out to grab the phone. She walked back in and handed it to her.

Before she turned it on, Alexis asked, "Mom, how come this phone works and it came from that time?"

"You are listening."

"Well, I got this phone later while we were traveling to Montana. The man who gave it to me was your father. Why it works is another story altogether. Now turn it on and say hello to your father."

Alexis' hands were shaking. She pressed the button and waited for the phone to come on. When it finally did, she saw a photo on the home screen of a young man with dark hair, a chiseled face and light green eyes. "Is this him?"

"That's your father."

"Oh my, he's so handsome."

"He was and charming too."

"Can I take this to bed with me?"

"Sure"

Alexis lay in bed staring at the photo of the man who was partly responsible for her existence. She couldn't believe it. She could hardly wait to hear about him and finally get to know him or as much as she could.

Abigail watched her fall asleep. Recalling those times were bittersweet, but Alexis needed to know. She just didn't want to break her heart, and eventually the stories would.

JOHN W. VANCE

ABOUT THE AUTHOR

John W. Vance is a former Marine and retired Intelligence
Analyst with the CIA. When not writing he spends as much
time as he can either with his family or in the water.
He lives in complete bliss where the waves meet the shore

For more information on
John W. Vance
visit
www.jwvance.com
www.facebook.com/authorjohnwvance

If you have time please leave a review on Amazon.

Thank you,
John W. Vance

Additional book by John W. Vance

CPSIA information can be obtained at www.ICGtesting.com
Printed in the USA
LVOW10s1918260615

444042LV00005B/388/P

9 781507 734162